William Sharpe

Humanity and the Man

William Sharpe

Humanity and the Man

ISBN/EAN: 9783337206550

Printed in Europe, USA, Canada, Australia, Japan

Cover: Foto ©Andreas Hilbeck / pixelio.de

More available books at **www.hansebooks.com**

BY

WILLIAM SHARPE, M.D., Q.U.I.,

ARMY MEDICAL DEPARTMENT ; AUTHOR OF "THE CONQUEROR'S DREAM AND OTHER POEMS."

~~~~~~~~~~~~~~

DUBLIN:

HODGES, FOSTER, AND FIGGIS.

LONDON:

SIMPKIN, MARSHALL, AND CO.

1878.

PREFACE.

In looking to the history of man, so far as it is known to us, we observe, that in his progress towards his present standard of civilisation, he seems to have entered upon, or passed through, four stages. In the first stage, as recorded in the Bible and supported by the authority of scientists, we find him of necessity placed in a tropical region, unclothed, exempt from manual labour, sustained by fruits, and living in a state of unconscious happiness; for his struggle for existence had not yet commenced. In the second stage, we find him clad in skins; removed from this paradise, and chiefly supported by the products of the chase;

A

yet not entirely so, for some few seem from an early date to have entered partially on the latter stages, namely, those of animal domestication and husbandry, soon to be adopted on a grand scale, and destined to supersede the hunter's phase, thenceforth to be followed only by unreclaimed and wandering tribes.

The poem, taking a short survey of these stages, deals chiefly with the continual struggle of mankind after a higher and more intellectual state of civilisation than it has yet attained, but towards which it is now fast approaching. It is based chiefly on the teachings of natural science, history, philosophy and Revelation, conveyed to a great extent in the form of allegorical and figurative representation; for the history of the Adamite, and the views of life which pass before him, represent, not only the progress of Humanity as a whole, but the course of any individual man of an original turn of mind struggling with the evils around him, and contending as it were for the mastery over himself, whilst groping his way through the dim and winding mazes of philosophy where he wanders in despair and doubt, till, the intuition of genius, as it were suddenly flashing across the dark wastes of sophistry and metaphysical disputation, dispels the gloom and sends him on his way; nor leaves him, till, like Prospero, he scales the heights to which he has aspired ; there henceforth to rest at peace, looking down upon the world from that high pinnacle of light and philosophic calm, which he, with so much difficulty attained.

" His visage drawn, he felt to sharp and spare ;
His arms clung to his ribs, his legs entwining
Each other, till, supplanted, down he fell
A monstrous serpent, on his belly prone,
Reluctant, but in vain ; a greater Power
Now ruled him, punished in the shape he sinned,
According to his doom.   He would have spoke,
But hiss for hiss returned with forked tongue
To forked tongue ; for now were all transformed.

Paradise Lost.

HUMANITY AND THE MAN.

BOOK I.

I SING of Life, Humanity and the Man,
Who first, of Heaven, from primal states upcalled,
To being awoke and human consciousness.
And prompted thus, or of the Muse inspired
Or Spirit taught, the narrative begins.
Within a vale, that as a garden smiled,
All unaccountable he found himself,
Not knowing why or whence he came, or how
Or whither bound, or what his destiny.
To north and east, encircling half its reach,
Impassable a chain of mountains rose,
Range upon range in air enormous piled
Until to heaven their towering cones upreared.
Afar to south the ocean spread serene ;
And divers lakes, fed from the hills, and crowned,
At intervals, with many a verdant isle,

B

Within the valley lay; and many a grove
Luxuriant, such as the Dryads love,
Was interspersed between : nor wanted there
Cascade or streamlet, mound or flowery lawn.
In keeping, too, with such fair scenes, th' abode
On earth of more than earthly bliss, were found
Giving them life, all brightest forms of air :—
Insects of sorts outrivalling in sheen
The radiance of the sun's great arch ; and birds
Of divers hues, of paradise well-named,
All azure, gold, purple, and snowy-white,
Discursive, flitting on the wing, at will,
In circles free or hovering 'mong the flowers,
Their downy plumes afloat upon the air,
Like mist condensed of parti-coloured light.
Spirits of heaven or habitants they seemed
Of brighter spheres, coming in guise of bird,
Prophetic heralds declaring fairer worlds
And higher states of being yet to be.
From wood to brake the voice of song resounds,
Joyous, from every trace of sorrow free.
And flowers of every brightest hue and kind
Lent lavishly their fragrance to the breeze.
Crowning the laden trees, all choicest fruits

Abundant there were found : and over all,
Pouring profuse from sun and golden cloud,
An ever-changing light unceasing played.

Long time in peace and blissful state, secure,
Roaming at large within this paradise,
The Man abode, and in existence joyed
Naught questioning, of life, the mysteries
Beyond his ken or causes intricate,
Until—sure sign of higher destiny—
Within his soul instinctively there sprang,
As though it were decreed the component
Co-ordinate of higher faculties,
A longing vague for something higher still,
Greater and grander than his present lot
Afforded him or than he here enjoyed.
And now, impelled as by necessity
Of higher law, there 's naught he will not dare
To satisfy this craving of the soul.
If only he the knowledge could attain
Of higher good and higher states of bliss,
The knowledge he, of evil, would essay.
And on this course he fully is resolved.
The tree, before him is, of knowledge placed,

Freely to taste ; the consequence foretold.
Rich, laden trees to tempt the appetite,
Which, ruled by reason, must in abstinence
Be tried, not gorged, culling before the time,
The fruits unripe of happiness reserved.
At present, irresponsible he stood—
Happy and blameless in the sight of Heaven ;
Happy, enjoying good, but in themselves,
Evil and good alike to him unknown.

In such like fitting mood, reason unheard,
Subordinate, and impulse at the helm,
The Tempter found him now.   As one who, trying
To steer a middle course 'twixt right and wrong,
Sways oft to either side, till force or chance
Or influence his balance overturns :
So swayed he then 'tween duty and desire,
Until, at length o'ercome, to serpent guile
He lent his ear, and unsuspecting fell,
Daring the evil, that he the good might know.
Forthwith, as though upon the sultry air,
Their drowsy spells Lethean odours cast,
Depression, langour, and a sense of weight,
And feeling as of dull forgetfulness

Absorbed his soul and sealed his eyes in sleep.
Then in the shadowy realms of dream involved,
The inward sense, of clogging substance freed,
Awakes to visions as of distant climes ;
Rocks, mountains, and untrodden solitudes,
Wide-spreading seas, primeval woods and dales,
And verdant plains and habitable tracts,
Where hunters roamed or civilisation spread.
But stranger still, wherever man was found,
A wondrous group before him ever rose :
A man, a woman, a serpent, and a child
At enmity were seen ; the former, fallen
Beneath the foe, were wounded unto death ;
The latter alone deadly the strife maintained.
The child, fearless and frank and innocent,
Love and immortal beauty breathing full,
Unaided then against the dragon stood.
The dragon, evermore with rage inflamed,
At thought of beauty, innocence, or love ;
But now with seven-fold fury filled at sight,
Surpassing aught by him aforetime seen
Or hitherto, of loveliness conceived,
His swollen crest with dreadful hiss upreared,
And tortuous, rolled his monstrous length in heaps,

And, gliding with a spiral motion, scaled
The eminence and coiled around the child,
And straight essayed to crush him in his folds.
Though hurt, the child with superhuman force
The monster seized, and hurled him stunned to earth,
Where long he writhed in agony and fear.
The scene was changed, and by a mighty flood
The group uprose; a woman with her child
Bewailed her husband by the dragon slain,
Dismembered there and drifted on the tide.
And changing 'gain, a multitude appeared,
And with them still, a woman and her child,
A man, now grown, a dragon and a cross.
Then far removed, in dim and distant lands,
The shifting group, incongruous was seen,
The same, but yet more vague and shadowy.
The dragon, too, more dreadful form assumed,
No longer vanquished, but triumphant now,
With fiendish rites and human sacrifice,
In monstrous shape, is worshipped as a God!
A god that still his worshippers devoured,
Till he and they evanished in the night!
Like one oppressed the sleeper groaned and sobbed,
For on his mind the changing vision palled;

Nor seemed to pass, but still persistent rose,
Nor could he guess the meaning or divine
The import sought therein to be conveyed.
But here a voice as from a distance called,
And to him said, or seemed at least to say :—
" Come ! I will show thee what so troubles thee ;
If thon canst understand, I will make known
The vision and the nature of the group."
With this he woke, and for a time believed
The voice still present, though he no one saw.

But now he felt the dawning consciousness
Of an approaching change : the ethereal flood
That erst in him to overflowing swelled,
And quick repelled from th' earthly mould all hurt,
All poisonous touch of noxious worm or plant,
Or gripe more fell of bodily disease,
Now dimmed by evil ineffectual flows,
Deprived of its once all-sufficing power.
No sooner has this inner change occurred,
Than dimmed his brow, and for the buoyancy
And strength, almost of spirit-life, he felt
Through every organ, every joint and limb,
Unusual langour steal, weakness untold,

And painful sense of lasting injury.
And simultaneous, too, strange doubts arise,
And fears as of impending dangers cloud
The mind, falling before, as lowering falls
The gloom of night when tempests gather round.
The knowledge now of evil he has gained,
And by experience knows, and good, but good
At distance far removed beyond his reach,
Unseen, or veiled in dim futurity.

With evil now, a life-long contest he
Must hold ; nor longer here in blissful state
Shall dwell secure, by fostering nature cared,
And every want supplied, but must henceforth,
Urged by the spur of sharp necessity,
Unaided, toil along life's arduous course.

Despondency upon his spirit fell
Thick, palpable as fall the shades of night,
No ray of light piercing the dark obscure ;
And in sad plight, wand'ring forlorn, he strayed
Till suddenly a Spirit before him stood,
Effulgent, shining in celestial robes,
And thus, with voice that rang clear as the tones

Of timbrel, lute, or golden harp began :
" Say whence has come this change deplorable,
This change alike of body, both, and mind ?
What cause has dimmed the lustre of thy soul ?
What hurt has it sustained or injury,
That thy whole nature by the shock is changed ?
Hast thou to appetite resigned thyself,
'Gainst reason's voice, impatient of delay ?
And hast thou sought, unguardedly, to obtain
' Forbidden knowledge by forbidden means ?'
Thou would'st be wise, but hast not taken care
To avoid the danger unto knowledge joined ;
And yet as gods thou wouldst omniscient be,
Ascend all heights, explore all depths, and scan
The searchless secrets of Infinity.
The first step thou hast gained : thou art as gods,
Knowing the good and evil, and as gods,
With each in turn thou must essay thy skill.
Support thy claim to fellowship with Heaven !
Evolve the good, the evil overcome.
No easy task or light work thou hast chosen,
But one that will thy utmost care demand.
Yet all the greater credit, thine ; for know
Henceforth in virtue of this knowlege gained,

In all things that concern thy welfare here,
And future destiny when hence removed,
Thou art co-labourer with the Deity !
Behoves thee now to take good heed and guard
With all thy might the treasure thou hast found ;
For its right use thou art responsible.
It is a talisman brings in its train
Evil and good ; if wrongly used or worse,
If prostituted to base ends by thee
Or thy posterity, it will entail
On them and thee incalculable woe :
Assuredly to intellect's lowest verge
The erring race shall fall ; deprived again
Of this, the gift of Heaven they so abused.
Then tottering here short time on ruin's brink,
Shall vanish from the earth, a hideous sight,
Unconscious of their state, reason's bright ray
By evil then within them all but quenched.
But if thou tend the gift with fostering care,
Expanding still, new glories 'twill unfold :
Ascending step by step, thou shalt in time
Attain to heights of knowledge now beyond
Conception's power or fancy's wildest dream !
The glorious harmonies of nature too,

To thee in part their beauties shall reveal ;
And thy soul glowing with kindred loveliness,
Shall recognise the Beautiful and thrill
With happiness, till then, to thee unknown.

Too rashly thou the enemy hast dared ;
Yet fret not that here in the first assault,
The Serpent, ancient type of evil decreed,
Has over thee a partial victory gained ;
For thou, in turn, against him shalt prevail,
And must, or yield, for freely hast thou chosen ;
And yet not freely, but as by constraint
Impelled to take this course, the only course
As yet laid down by which thou can'st attain
To higher destiny : as the pure ore,
Purged of its dross, has through the furnace come ;
So through the evil, or what seems it, lies
The only way to higher states of good.
Grieve not that this is so ; for rest assured,
All things throughout the boundless universe
Are ordered right : whatever is, is best.
With courage therefore set about thy task,
Promote the good, the evil counteract.
A noble task withal, and one besides,

Thy toil with interest fully will repay,
When time shall be ; for henceforth know thou art
A conscious Traveller through Eternity ;
And in thy several grades and states of being,
Co-worker with the Deity ordained.
Thou also shalt create for thine own good.
But see, that all thy work be genuine,
And bear the stamp of truth ; all else is vain
And will not stand, or worse, will work thee woe.
But hence, depart, and find thee other home,
For here, within this vale, as heretofore,
By nature cared, no longer shalt thou dwell
Nor shall return ; necessity forbids.
Henceforth by thine own labour shalt thou live.
Begin and persevere and overcome.
Compel the earth to give thee of her fruits ;
And hold, as lord, dominion o'er her tribes ;
So shalt thou raise another paradise,
Where bliss shall dwell, and knowledge free to all,
Shall yield her stores of intellectual food.
But steep is the ascent and long the way
That thou must tread, ere at the goal arrived ;
Dangers await at every turn besides,
And blinding fogs thy vision shall obscure.

Yet see, the while, that thou persist, for light
Piercing the dark shall oft thy steps illume—
Light such as thou art fitted to receive.
At first truth veiled in allegory in part
Shall be conveyed ; but as the mind expands,
In literal form direct shall be revealed.
For like a child, with simplest rudiments,
Thou must begin ; all other modes are vain.
Go, persevere, and bear in mind that thou
Art placed on trial of thy fitness for
Promotion hence to higher state or sphere.
And such as I am, such thou too shalt be,
And greater far in time's revolving course ! "

So spake the Seraph, and abrupt withdrew,
As he had come.   His words deep impress made,
And with fresh hope the Traveller they inspired.
And so, in turn, he went upon his way.
Yet sorrowed much, his early home to leave,
And wander forth unfriended and unknown.
He wept with sense of loneliness o'ercome ;
But soon new scenes and th' urgent wants of life
Demanding toil, his sorrowing tears dispelled.

'Twas in such mood with resolution fixed
To persevere, the Traveller journeyed on
Through distant lands and regions desolate.
At length he reached far in the middle waste
A point where all seemed suddenly to change.
He entered there a deep secluded dell,
A long defile that wound its gloomy course
Remote among the mountain solitudes.
Beneath the rude cliffs and the rocks he passed,
That all in ruinous confusion piled
O'erlook'd the glen, as there, vast, motionless,
Crag, pinnacle, and precipice they stood,
In all the vague varieties of form
Which revelling fancy on the outline grafts;
Embattled tower, colossal head or bust,
Memnon or Sphinx by hand of nature framed,
Vaster than e'er Egyptian king designed,
Or priest, to guard the temple of his gods !
At intervals were found, deep-tangled clumps
Of undershrub, thickly with berries laden;
Besides more stately growths of branching palm,
Of oak or mountain ash, which lent their shade,
Grateful at times, against the noonday sun,
As by the marge of crystal pool they stood

Reflected clear, or by the founts that welled
From 'neath the rocks or streams that hasted down
The hilly slopes, collecting from above.
With wonder and a sense of awe he gazed
Upon the heights and towering pinnacles
That round him rose, diversified and vast.
With new delight each point he scans and climbs
Each rocky ridge and spur and wide explores
The secretest recesses of the dell.
But like a man on pleasure all intent,
Unsatisfied with what he has obtained,
His path direct within the glen he leaves
To stray among the mountain solitudes,
That with false show attract his erring steps.

Then straight, intending to return full soon,
He sought what easiest path offered ascent
Or mountain gorge presenting gradual slope,
This to pursue, until the brow was passed.
Height after height with difficulty he gains ;
But gained in turn, still other heights succeed,
What seemed the last, illusive from below,
Tempting to the ascent, which seen by him
At first, had been abandoned in despair,

A task impossible ; but thus displayed,
By halves in part, unwitting draw him on,
Until, amid the mountain ranges hemmed,
He lost his way, and sought in vain return.
Perplexed, and with keen sense of danger urged,
From point to point, by hill and strait he went,
And rocky steep, still desperate to regain
The dell, when suddenly upon the brink
Of hanging rock or precipice he came.
Disclosed beneath, a horrid gulf, a rift,
As if the shattered mountain had disjoined ;
All natural objects shrank to smallest size
In the dim distance seen ; rock-rooted pines
Or giant oaks dwindled to undershrub ;
The very sounds like dreamy echoes there
Rose indistinct and languid from below :
And full in front, from upper ranges drawn,
A mighty torrent foamed impetuous down
Its rocky bed, tumbling in snowlike heaps,
Till, thundering, o'er the broken ledge it swept,
Shooting within an arch of purple and gold
Into the abyss aneath the cloven hills.
Spell-bound upon the ravine's verge he lay
At once attracted and alarmed, for now

Both awe and wonder in his breast combined.
Emboldened then he sought if any strait,
Among the cliffs, might lead into the gorge,
By which perchance he might regain the vale.
But slow descending from the frigid hills,
The creeping fogs advance, till rocks and gulfs
And cataracts, in the same darkness veiled,
Above, beneath, around him lie unseen,
But in his thoughts more terrible become,
For shuddering here at every step he fears
Downwards into the dark abyss to fall,
Or on the horrid brink he seems to stand,
Clings to the rock, or strives convulsively
To reach the top or find some surer hold ;
While strained imagination paints below,
Impaling crags and caves and cliffs and chasms.
So struggled he on ruin's brink, beyond
All human aid, and darkness round him closed.
Meanwhile, the ghastly promptings of despair
And horrid shapes on every side assail
With dark suggestions, urging him to seek
A refuge in the death, he would avoid.

But at this pass, again the Seraph came,

C

All radiant still, but milder than before ;
Compassion, tenderness, and charity
Sat on his countenance, shone in his eyes,
Or trembled on his tongue, as thus he spake :—
"Ah ! wretched ! wherefore didst thou, erring, leave,
To wander here, thy destined course prescribed.
Enough of dangers there awaited thee,
And toils, but toils proportioned to thy strength,
Not greater, and such as thou might'st, withal,
By perseverance, have in time o'ercome ;
But these, beneath which now thou should'st have
     fallen,
Thou soughtest out; not on thee were imposed.
Yet fear not now, for nobly hast thou done,
Nobly hast toiled ; what mortal could, thou didst.
Come ! follow me ! henceforth I am thy guide,
And will to thee, as we proceed, unfold
Whatever is expedient thou should'st know.
Things past, things present, and to come, in part
Thou shalt behold ; let this suffice, nor seek
To compass more. So saying he led the way.

BOOK II.

THENCE easily by easy gradients soon,
Among the hills, they reached a narrow pass,
The entrance to a wide extended plain,
Which stretched afar to north and west, and merged
Into a waste and barren wilderness,
Where a dim light, like twilight, ever seemed ;
Rocks, fens, and moors beneath the lowering sky,
And mould'ring ruins, all desolate, and hemmed
By dismal tracts and floods of Acheron,
That lay remote, and into darkness passed.
Upon the plain a mighty multitude,
A motley crowd of divers tongues appeared,
Took form, emerging, as it were, from night
And darkness into light, and wandering moved
To and fro a time, or seemed to move, as on
They sped towards the desert shores beyond :
Again to vanish there from mortal sight,
To vanish there, but not the less to be !

Among the first, a stalwart Race appeared,
That warred with nature, and by shrewd device
Compelled the earth to yield her hidden stores ;
And by the right of conquest soon obtained,
And held, in full, dominion o'er her tribes,—
Fish, fowl, and beast of whatsoever kind,
All things that lived and moved upon the earth,
Were found in air, or in the waters dwelt.
But here contemporaneously was seen,
On central ground, uprising in the midst,
A structure vast, laid down exact by square
And rule, and in the outline seemed alike
For strength designed and durability.
And in the haze and distance there appeared
On every side, far as the eye could reach,
A multitude, uncultured, fierce, and wild ;
Hunters they seemed, who lived improvident
From day to day on what the chase supplied.

Whereupon his guide, the Traveller, thus addressed :
" What means that structure with the central few,
That near it dwell ?   What mean the crowds remote,
That stand aloof, dispersed o'er all the plains,
Grow indistinct, and in the distance fade ? "

To whom, in turn, the Seraph then replied :
" The scattered multitudes thou see'st are those,
That shall to men in future time be known
As earth's primeval habitants, the first
Unto extinction doomed of Heaven's decree,
The penalty for nature's laws transgressed.
Even now the crisis comes ! behold how dark
The heavens ! destruction teems on high ! their
    doom
Descends amain with cataclysmal swoop.
But, left unto themselves, they reck not yet,
The death that nears, or fate that o'er them hangs ;
Deprived, in greater part, of Heaven's high gift,
The gift of intellect they so abused,
Employing it in fabricating lies
And snares, and in devising darkest deeds
Of infamy, of treachery and wrong,
To the dictates of envy, malice, hate,
Self-interest, revenge, or lust of blood !
Deprived of intellect's celestial beams,
They blindly drive, and recognise not now
The warning signs placed in the angry sky.

" On th' other hand, the central few thou see'st,

Of nobler type, are those who have not quenched
Within themselves this light of Heaven, vouchsafed,
Or have not fallen from their true estate.
The warning signs disclosed on high, they see
And understand, and timely have prepared
Them fitting means of safety and escape
Against the day of wrath pronounced and doom.
The ark, that stately rises in the midst,
To man and beast protection shall afford—
Protection adequate to all who seek
Their refuge there, and shall throughout all time
Be held a sacred symbol and a type
For evermore of safety to mankind,
An emblem of that mighty ark designed
To fill the earth, that edifice wherein
Thenceforth the human family shall dwell
Secure against the floods and storms of change.

" Discernest thou, now gathering in haste
From every side, what divers creatures throng
Into the ark ; from all the lower tribes
Select they come, and man's protection seek ;
Creatures alike by Providence ordained ;
Their bounds prescribed according to His will,

And stations in the scale of being fixed.
Submissive to the Patriarch they come,
Of every kind, chosen by rule laid down,
Of seven or two, as they by outward mark
Or sign, clean or unclean are designate.
Now recognise in the selection made,
And in the ark itself, discern the type
Of perpetuity, from change exempt ;
The rising dawn of a new order of things
Not subject to the fickle rules of chance.
Behold in it Domestication's course,
And Civilisation's growth, thenceforth designed
To supersede the Hunter's nomad life
Precarious, and now inadequate
To meet the needs and rising wants of man.
No more by hard necessity impelled,
And hunger's pangs, shall he, the chase, pursue,
Driving to dark extermination's verge.
Henceforth all creatures of whatever kind,
Clean or unclean, according to their worth,
Shall under man's protection come, and care.
The clean in greater numbers shall be had :
Nor shall there any creature, great or small,
Beast, bird, or creeping thing in the great scale

Of life, exterminated be, or struck
From out the chain by Providence decreed ;
But all shall have their right to live allowed,
Their place allotted, and their bounds prescribed,
Their numbers fixed, as heretofore they were,
By nature's laws, imposed with due regard
Unto the common weal, ere man disturbed
The balance just, which now he must restore."

So spake the Seraph, when darkness for a time
Involved the plain, sealing from mortal sight
All objects there, as though they had not been,
Or were in sleep, the coinage of the soul,
Called up and formed within the realms of dream.
So seemed the vision thus from view withdrawn ;
And so the coming, for darkness now removed,
Far on the wide and billowy plain they see
The ark immense of civilisation spread,
Where roamed at large the hunter tribes untamed,
Which now had vanished from the plain ; and yet
Not wholly, for some wand'ring forms remained,
Still blending with the scene, dim, indistinct,
Like shadows on the far horizon's verge.

And now, continuing, the Seraph said :—
" Behold straightway new complications rise,
New dangers, difficulties, and toils upspring ;
Evils before unknown—or rather known,
The same unchanged, but in new dress arrayed,
As meet—shall still gigantic shapes assume,
Shall still assert their old prerogative,
As erst, with good eternally to war.
Yet they no more shall triumph as of late,
They did, involving man in world-wide ruin,
Decay and death ; but in their limits now,
More circumscribed, shall work the fall of states ;
And in their train bring pestilence and war,
Bondage, oppression, tyranny, and chains,
And servitude of every lowest kind.
And lo ! they come. See in the vineyard there
Decreed, the lower shall the higher serve ;
At once the cause and the effect revealed :
The curse, " Servant of servants shalt thou be,"
Pronounced by Noah 'gainst his younger son,
Embodies both, and in the outline shows
The second movement retrograde, of man,
Uprising now in civilisation's course,
And ending not, as heretofore in death,

But slavery of a section of his race.
Unto his sons the Patriarch bequeaths
A noble art—the art of husbandry ;
An art from which flows universal good,
But from which also, when in turn abused,
A partial evil springs, as here descried :
An evil, in the main, characterised
By darkened intellect and low desires,
Depravity and want of moral tone ;
All self-respect and innate sense of shame
Lost or impaired, till finally the man,
No longer guided by the light of truth,
Reason or intellect, degraded sinks
Below the standard of humanity :
Nature imprinting on the outward form
The vitiated likeness of the soul—
The soul that vivifies, pervades, and moulds
After its image man's material frame.
And hence the men, by nature's law enforced,
Who are unfit, themselves aright, to rule,
Or their affairs to guide, must straight descend
To slavery or vanish from the scene.

" Next on the plains, behold conquest and war,

And fierce oppression's iron rule commence :—
The plains of Shinar where great Babel lifts
Her stately towers, presumptuous, to the skies,
Essaying the empire of the world to bring
Under the sway of Nimrod or his line ;
Till frustrate by new dialects and tongues,
Language diverse, tending to the uprise
Of different nationalities, dispersed,
Without cohesion 'mong themselves or bond ;
Impossible to bind in concord, fixed
Under one head ; and hence the blasted towers
Of Babel stand, a sign of broken rule,
Secession from the throne by Nimrod raised.

"The builders here dispersed, prepare to see
Westward afar, upon a fertile plain,
Beside a noble stream, Nilus, renowned
Throughout the world, a mighty empire grow ;
Behold Egyptus, else Mizraem called,
The home of art, where early science springs,
And mystic lore, cognizant of the laws
Of force, of matter, and of spirit, attains
To power, and to the knowledge of things beyond
The bounds of earth. Knowledge there handed down,

By symbols slowly, and by secret rites,
And words of mouth after fit trials passed :—
Trials, and ceremonies, and types imposed,
The tests alike of intellectual power,
Force, courage, and integrity of mind ;
To Wisdom, Strength, and Beauty still allied,
Or the prerogative of these combined ;—
These the great pillars of the universe
Of import vast a mystic meaning bear ;
And in contradistinction stand to evil,
Characterised in turn by ugliness,
Unwisdom, weakness, and deformity.
For by the trial ceremonies enforced,
The wordly-minded are excluded still
From knowledge of the higher truths, which they,
Seeing in part, see not :— truth which displayed
In clearer form, they would corrupt and change ;
Till finally the whole obscured and quenched
Should in oblivion sink, or shadow-like,
Stand lingering in some fantastic show,
Like the disjointed fragments of a dream !
And, lo ! too soon this downward change occurs.
See now what mass of fables, crude and wild,
Have risen the intellect of man to cloud,

Till, darkened all or turned awry for gain
Or love of power, it straight distorts the light,
Or misinterprets else for selfish aim
The meanings of each sign, until removed
In time, the shadow for the substance stands.
Symbols, that erst the Deity revealed
In close connexion with the universe,
And man's position in the scale of life,
Now changed and multiplied, are in their turn
Worshipped as gods with vain and slavish rites.

" But ere the change or climax passed, behold
Provision made, that still the truth may live
Preserved in stony record in the works
That rise, erected in this wondrous clime,
The chosen museum of the world, where nought
Material ever seems to fade or change ;
Where every nobler fabric raised by man
Eternal stands, defying still the siege
Of time, exerted elsewhere through the breath
Of slow decay, or frost, or mouldering damp ;
But here forbidden to intrude, debarred
By the decree of Heaven's Eternal King.
Such records in those mighty works are placed

In temples, statues, tombs, and pyramids.
There greeting still with mellow notes the dawn,
Great Memnon's statue stands, herald of change
From written hieroglyphic signs abstruse,
To vocal sounds in facile marks conveyed ;
And silent there the solemn Sphinx reclines,
Her awe-inspiring form invested full,
As with the power and might of him who called
From night, and in the living rock revealed
The monstrous offspring born of intellect
In wedlock joined to animality :
Of intellect from reason there divorced,
And under sway of animal impulse.
From age to age the mystic idol stands,
Its riddle still propounding to mankind,
And shall propound until the end of time,
Condemning all who fail to read aright,
Or rather in their practice fail to solve
The higher truth, the mystery conceals.

" All these, besides, a history in themselves,
Corroborative evidence shall afford
Unto the spoken or the written word.
For lo ! what exodus of Sages now

Go forth to teach, dispersed to north and east,
Who shall the truth preserve, imparting it,
Though much obscured, unto the nations round.
Fit centres, they, of civilisation there
Shall find, wherein to found academies
And schools of art, that shall surpass the old.
Egypt's philosophy, abstruse, reserved,
In Greece shall meet a more congenial soil,
Untrammelled there by strict hierarchal law,
A higher flight and wider scope shall gain ;
For at this time Urania shall descend,
Divinely stooping from her heavenly sphere,
And there on earth the torch of genius light—
Light with her own transcendent loveliness ;
Until her votaries enraptured burn,
Filled with conceptions of the Beautiful
By sympathy mysterious instilled :
Beauty, however, expressed in song or sounds
Harmonious or symmetries of form—
Of form, that fixed in parian stone, shall stand,
In outward mould, the rival of herself,
In grace divine, in matchless symmetry.
Genius, her minister and spouse, ordained
To stand between her and the multitude,

And sway their minds, that she to them may yield
Some leaven of her own celestial life,
Some measure of her loveliness, inspired
By contemplation of the good and true,
That they, thereby, her lovers may become,
And grow themselves by Heaven's eternal will,
To be in time, what they admired and loved,
A race on earth of gods and goddesses,
Of higher worlds the habitants elect,
Fairer than fair Olympian deity !
Or Nymph or Naid of the wood or stream !

" Yet ere the flight of time, rolling from out
Eternity, such heavenly change bring forth,
Vast preparations are being made, that then
Not only Greece alone the good shall know,
But all the nations kindred of the earth
Shall share alike if they are worthy found.
Behold a chosen people now go up,
Versed in Egyptian arts, from Egypt's realm,
Where they have sojourned in adversity,
And were in bondage kept and servitude,
Unto a land, the land of Canaan named,
An heritage unto their fathers given,

To Abram, Isaac, Israel, and his sons,
Whose seed they are. Up through the wilderness
By route circuitous they march, as led
By Moses, Aaron, and the son of Nun,
Following the cloudy pillar advanced before,
An emblem of that spiritual light, ordained
To guide man through the wilderness of life.
Slowly they march under fixed laws enforced
Severe, the tests of their obedience due ;
And ceremonies imposed, as though they were
Being trained in this their early nomad life,
That they may enter on a higher phase,
A civilisation more advanced and state
More permanent, what time they shall become
The owners of the promised heritage.
Thus in their course, in vivid light, is drawn
An outline of the history of mankind ;
For slow through trials and adversities
Shall be the progress of humanity.
But still no power shall hold the higher man
In slavery, or shall obstruct his course.
Despite of numbers and advantage held
The lower still before him shall give way.

D

" Lo ! they, too, in the wilderness construct
An ark, designed in fashion of the first,
A type of that wherein man refuge found—
A symbol ever sacred to his race,
In which is laid the laws he must observe,
If he his future welfare, would ensure.
See also in the golden cherubims
With wings outspread over the mercy-seat,
Is shadowed forth the progress of mankind,
And man's election to a higher sphere
Slowly advanced from lower grade by law
Immutable according to desert.
And further, in those sacrificial rites
Is shadowed forth the war of Evil and Good
Conjointly in their action on mankind
Under th' eternal laws of Heaven prescribed.
To war with Good is the sole aim of Evil,
To war eternally, essaying still
With deadly touch or influence malign
To wound to death or injure and deform.
Hence is the Serpent type of Evil chosen,
The grand appropriate type of Evil; for
Low'st of that Class, or Plan ideal of which
Man is the head, the footless Serpent stands,

Low, subtle, loathsome, venemous, and prone ;
Deprived of outward limbs, and forced to crawl,
Degraded, in the dust, but armed instead
As with the fangs of death itself, the signs
External set of inbred hellish hate.
The bleeding victim shows the doom incurred
Of that, which under th' operation comes
Of evil through sin, and the atonement made
For law with death, is ever satisfied.
Death is the natural result of evil,
Or of the imperfections caused thereby ;
For imperfections of themselves denote
Deformity or injuries received ;
And nature ever hastens to expunge,
Striking forthwith from out the sum of life
Whatever being is imperfect found.
The sacrificer, by the rite, proclaims
The law unchangeable of death imposed,
And, by the offered substitute, declares
That he, himself, is tainted and condemned.
But in the substitute perfection, still,
As matter of necessity, is enjoined ;
For only by perfection can the power
Of death ever be finally o'ercome.

Hence is the sacrifice at once a type
Of death, the forfeit penalty incurred
Under the law, and of redemption found,
Redemption by Perfection wrought in full,
The work of one more perfect Man, ordained
For all to die, a final Sacrifice ;
A voluntary offering given, that He
For ever may the sting of Death uproot ;
For Death over Perfection hath no power.
A voluntary offering made for man,
That man through Him a higher life may gain--
A higher life—the gift of boundless love !
Of love, the fount whence all perfections flow,
The source of Beauty, Life, and Energy,
Th' Eternal Word—Soul of the universe !
And first offspring of Deity begotten !"

BOOK III.

So spake the Seraph fully, and explained
Unto the Traveller still where aught abstruse
Or difficult to understand appeared,
As thus before them passed the leading points,
That form on earth the history of man.
And now continuing said : " Yet for a time
I shall discuss what passes in review,
As though it were by narrative revealed :
But afterwards it will be adequate
For thee to see, for thou shalt understand
The greater part, without the aid of words.

" Now as the period of probation passed,
And trial, the sons of Israel are enjoined
To take possession of the Promised land,
The heritage by right of conquest theirs,
What time by force of arms they shall succeed

In driving out, such is the will of Heaven,
From all their holds, the aboriginal tribes,
Degenerate vile, and so of Heaven condemned
To be cast out or held in slavery,
According to the sentence on them passed,
Their due, by nature's law impartial fixed.
Slowly in civilisation they advance :
Some cities found, some clear the wooded tracts,
Plant and reclaim or cultivate the fields,
Labouring assiduously both for their own
And for the nation's weal. All serve one cause,
And are obedient to one common law :
The law of Moses in the ark contained,
Treasured and guarded with religious awe,
As the sole testament in which are sealed
The terms of compact which they must observe,
Which, while observed, protection is vouchsafed.
Thus they a time in brotherhood shall dwell
And primitive simplicity, still ruled
And guided by their elder's voice in all,
Or judged at intervals by fitting men,
Prophets and seers, of Heaven, still inspired,
Till, with the growth of wealth, corruptions grow,
And with corruptions tyranny and wrong,

Outrage and strife, and poverty and crime :
Judgments shall in the main be bought and sold ;
And all the land shall groan, oppressed until,
Beyond endurance tried, the people rise
Unanimous, and cry, ' Give us a king,
That he may rule us like the nations round.'

" Thus, then, in time, theocracy shall change
To kingly government, corruption's cure
Or punishment, for all shall serve the king,
And yet thereby more liberty shall gain
If he be just, and competent to rule.
So is the change itself, of Heaven designed
For higher ends, a blessing in the mean ;
For now development shall grow apace,
And arts and national prosperity ;
For he, if he be such as Heaven ordains,
Shall as a father guard his people's rights,
Grieve with their grief, and in their joy rejoice.
Hence is the prophet Samuel now enjoined
To seek them out a king ; and Saul is chosen,
Fittest to rule, a man of seeming worth ;
But, after trial made, is wanting found :
Thence cast aside, rejected.   And, again,

The prophet unto Bethlehem is sent
To choose a king. Before him in review
The sons of Jesse pass : of these, Eliab
The fairest seems ; and him he would anoint,
Unwittingly, for one he has not seen ;
But is restrained therefrom, till David come,
The youngest who, of none account, still keeps
His father's flock, contented with his state,
With nature and himself communing deep ;
Before the prophet now he comes, a youth
Shapely and fair and comely to behold,
And Samuel here anointed him with oil,
King over Israel, and the head to be   .
Of a long line of princes and of kings,
The Minstrel King, favoured of Heaven; from whom,
In latter days, a royal son shall spring,
A sovereign-prince, the Christ who shall obtain
The sceptre and the monarchy of earth.

" But, 'gainst the advent of that glorious time,
Long preparation must be made and change
Concomitant in nations wide apart,
That all mankind, both Jews and Gentiles then,
May reap the benefit, progressing still,

Until, united in the bonds of love,
They dwell in peace and lasting fellowship.
But first long centuries of mutual war,
And tyranny and bloodshed must elapse.
Conquest and war, an evil both, and scourge,
Which man's condition oft necessitates ;
And so necessitated, still shall lead
To good and save him from a lower fall ;
For in proportion to his innate worth,
His love of truth and sense of right and wrong,
Shall he precedence take, and overcome,
Holding the reigns of sovereignty ;
For nature still the higher people calls
To rule, and to that end endoweth them
With courage, strength, and intellectual power.

" Under their chosen prince united now,
The Israelites another stage advance ;
David the Shepherd King, a minstrel born,
And soldier by necessity constrained,
Leads them to war against their enemies,
And, by his prowess and heroic deeds
And high example set, inflames their minds,
Enkindling in the breast of each a love

Of martial fame, that victory still ensured,
Till one by one the bordering nations are
Subdued and spoiled and tributary made.
And now, war laid aside, the land has rest,
And turns, enriched to internal display,
To civilisation and the arts of peace.
Colossal works of architecture soon
Arise, and under Solomon attain
Their highest pitch ; walled cities, palaces
And the great temple of Jerusalem famed,
The wonder of the world, and unsurpassed
Elsewhere or equalled by the works of man,
As fitting such an edifice should be,
Wherein is reached the culminating point
Of that first system of religion spread
Throughout the world, here only pure upheld,
As Heaven inspired, with solemn pomp and rites
Mysterious, that symbolised in one,
Man's fall, his judgment and the atonement found.

" The climax reached in opulence and power,
Reaction straight sets in ; dissensions rise
And feuds ; ten tribes secede from David's throne
And lapse into idolatry, befooled

By wicked kings to bow to wood and stone ;
Until at length demoralised and fallen,
They are, as slaves, led captive and dispersed.
The men of Judah hold by David's line,
Retaining still the temple as their right,
And stronghold of Jerusalem, the seat
Of empire fixed. The tribe of Judah now
A varied fortune shall attend and guide,
As with th' unerring reins of destiny,
Through every change of man's eventful being.
They, too, ofttimes forsaking Israel's God,
To heathen worship turn, seeking to spirits
Impure, to Moloch, Baal, and Ashtoreth,
And to their idols grim, uncouth upreared
In groves select, by hill or fountain side,
Until recalled by chastisement severe,
By foreign yoke, by famine or the sword :
Or unrepentent or inveterate, still
Holding to their idolatries accurst,
Are unto Babylon twice captive led,
Prisoners of war, their city overthrown,
And there detained, till Cyrus sets them free.

" But here meanwhile, repenting of their sins,

And roused unto a knowledge of their state,
A mission they unconciously fulfil.
Through them th' Almighty now unto the world,
His purposes to manifest, begins,
And providence more fully to make known,
Till that, in the fulness of time, the work
Of Satan, He for ever shall annul,
And lead mankind from darkness into light.
The noblest of the Hebrew youths are chosen,
That they, instructed in Chaldean lore,
And reconciled unto their lot, become
Thenceforth th' adopted children of the state,
And faithful, serve the government in all ;
Nor shall responsible positions now,
Or highest offices or posts of honour
From any be withheld, provided that,
In course of time, they competent are found :
So wills the king of Babylon, whose word
Is law, that he thereby more firmly may
The basis of the Chaldean empire fix,
But Heaven meanwhile far otherwise decrees ;
For lo ! the princes of the Hebrews still,
Though tried and faithful servants of the king,
Preserve intact their nationality.

They will not with the Babylonians blend,
Nor will they join in their religious rites,
Before their idols to prostrate themselves.
Baffled in this, the king, enraged, will force
Them to conform, or disobedient will
To swift destruction doom them, obstinate,
And straight commands, that if they fall not down
In humble adoration of his gods,
And idols on the plain of Duro set,
What time the sound of dulcimer they hear,
Sackbut or psaltery, to worship call,
They, of a certainty, the self-same hour
Into a fiery furnace shall be thrown.
But they, in mind resolved, compliance still
Refuse, setting at naught the king's decree,
Who now incensed with indignation caused,
That they, the furnace seven times more should heat,
And Shadrach, Meshach, and Abed-nego
Then cast therein, in coats aud hosen bound.
Forthwith these men are in the furnace thrown,
For now the king's commands brook no delay.
But they, in spirit clad, walk in the flames
Unhurt, secure, as though they walked at noon
In regal court, in grotto, or in bower.

Whereon the king astounded and amazed,
Dismay and horror on his countenance,
Uprose in haste and called them forth by name.
Such their triumph, that in Chaldea then
Its first death-wcund idolatry received,
And now with honours laden, and rewards,
They are remanded to their seats again
As rulers in th' affairs of Babylon.

" Thus they, expert in all Chaldean art,
Advance in worldly affluence and power,
Preserving their religion still and laws,
Until what time they are again returned
Unto Jerusalem, as now advised
By Daniel, greatest of the Hebrew seers,
A man beloved of Heaven, to whom is shown
By vision strange of complex animals,
He-goat or Ram, creatures of divers mould,
From the four winds successively uprisen,
The rise and fall of monarchies, until
The consummation of the primal phase,
And change thenceforth to a new order of things.
The Mede and Persian, Greek and Roman play
Their several parts, ushering the coming dawn,

And fitting preparations make against
Th' advent of Him, to whom the shadowy forms
Of sacrificial expiations point,
And, worship 'mong the Jews and Gentiles spread,
With all th' idolatries upraised thereon
A superstructure vast, wide as the earth,
Now to its centre being sapped and shaken, '
That it in time be finally overthrown.

"But now the Hebrews, to their land returned,
Begin once more Jerusalem to rebuild,
And Solomon's great temple to restore.
Idolatry with its degrading rites,
Abominations false and slavish found,
For ever they discard, and pride themselves
Thereon, thinking that now they cannot err.
But once increased in opulence and power,
New evils come ; dissenting factions rise,
Divers denominations, orders, sects,
Self-righteous pharisees, austere and proud,
Scribes, doctors, and expounders of the law
Priests, tyrants, who the crown of David snatch ;
All, seeking still by every means their own
And not the nation's weal, embroil the land ;

Their country's enemies, insensate, doomed
In punishment, to work her final ruin,
And bring therewith destruction on themselves

" The nation, by contending factions torn,
Is made the home of every violence,
The haunt of vices more debasing far,
Than all the crude idolatries of old.
Pride, falsehood, ever-gnawing envy, hate,
Hypocrisy, all-grasping avarice,
Corruption, outrage, tyranny, and strife,
On either hand, increasing still abound,
Until the State, no longer capable
Of civil government or management
Of its affairs, succumbs to outer force,
Obliged to yield its forfeit liberty
To Rome ; a province now annexed thereto,
And made amenable to Roman law,
By which contending factions are restrained,
Restrained indeed, but otherwise unchanged ;
Nay rather much more obdurate become,
Expecting, as they do, the advent now
Of Israel's hope, Messiah, long foretold
In holy writ, about this time to appear ;

In whom they hope to find a temporal king,
A worldly conqueror who shall vengeance take
On all their foes, unworthy though they are.
But who appears far other than they expect,
A babe, of none account, in manger born,
A lowly child of Bethlehem, whose birth
Is only announced unto a chosen few,
Attested by a star in th' East uprisen,
And angel choirs, by simple shepherds, heard
Hosannas singing, as by night they watch.
But whom, now unto manhood grown, still less
Will they accept, not finding what they sought
A man solely on martial exploits bent,
Who shall make good his title, and the crown
Of Judah win, as David's rightful heir,
By deeds accomplished worthy of their prince.
Yet failing this, or not inclined thereto,
His mission they with rancour will reject ;
And do reject insultingly, though vouched
For by display of superhuman powers,
And miracles now openly performed ;
Besides His other more than human gifts,—
Innate command, unrivalled intellect,
Wisdom and worth and charity and love

E

Visibly expressed in every lineament,   .
In outward mould, in symmetry or form,
In grace divine, perfection absolute :
The grand ideal archetype of Heaven
Embodied here ; in whom alone mankind,
Imperfect else, have reached perfection now.
But good by evil ever is opposed,
And all the more, the greater the extremes ;
Transcendent good in darker natures naught
But envy excites and hate proportional.
Hence the Messiah now, to their own loss,
The Jews reject ; for evil still is blind,
Advancing oft the good it would oppose,
With grievous pain redounding on itself,
And chastisement and retribution dire.
But unto Him come as many as are given,
That seeing, they may see, and hearing hear ;
And whom enlightened, He enlightens more,
According to their need ; and whom, He will,
Selects, His chosen ministers, that they,
Throughout the world, His mission may declare.

" Thus He on earth His ministry completes,
And nigh th' accomplishment thereof ascends,

As heretofore, the Mount of Olivet,
And thence, the downfall of Jerusalem notes
With pain ; for He alone of all her sons
Beholds her coming doom ; and there makes known
To His Beloved, what of the future they
Should know ; and more especially what time,
His followers should from the city flee,
In haste dispersed, her judgments to escape.

" But now, scribe, pharisee, and priest, all sects,
Whose evil deeds His teaching still denounced,
Inflamed with rage, occasion seek whereby
To accuse Him ; and false witnesses suborn
In their behoof, on points touching their law.
Him then they seize, in Gethsemane betrayed ;
And to the palace of Caiaphas straight
They bring Him, and interrogate Him, till
The high priest cried in wrath, ' What need we more ?
Have we not heard His blasphemy avowed ?
Away with Him unto the judgment-seat.'
And to the judgment-seat in Pilate's hall,
They led Him bound.   But Pilate, seeing no evil
In Him, and knowing for envy they had seized
The Christ, the man of Galilee so called,

Will liberate Him from their hold ; but they,
Incensed the more, cry out with one accord ;—
' No ! no ! rather release the robber chief !
We will not have the Nazarene ! Away
With Him to Calvary ; He stands arraigned
For blasphemy, and by our law must die !
Away with Him ! We will not have this man
To rule over us : henceforth we have no king
But Cæsar ; and, who makes himself a king,
Is Cæsar's enemy ; wilt thou therein
Assist ? If so beware the consequence.'
Thus they outcry, until sedition drowned
The voice of justice ; for self-interest here
With Pilate weighed, and craven fear so wrought.
That he to death the innocent condemns,
Against his better judgment, to appease
The fury of the hireling crowd, by priests
And pharisees seditiously suborned.

"The Saviour, now committed to their hands.
To Calvary they lead, and Golgotha,
The place of horrors dire, with human bones
And blood defiled, and Golgotha thence named.
And there, Him to th' accursed tree they nail,

Despitefully, with malefactors joined ;
And from the earth uplift Him, wantonly
Exposed to the revilings of the crowd,
Who taunt Him now in bitterest mockery.
But He, His mission to fulfil, endures
Until the end, the wrath upon Him poured,
Then bows His head submissively and dies !
Earth feels the shock and to her centre reels ;
The heavens withhold their light ; all nature groans
Ill-omened darkness o'er Jerusalem hangs ;
The shrouded dead, bursting their cerements,
Arise and in the holy city walk
Disquieted : of greater moment too
Than all,—within the Temple of Solomon
The veil, itself from top throughout is rent ;
The veil, symbol ordained of secrecy,
That until now, before the sanctuary stood,
Concealing still the holy place from sight
Profane, or vulgar gaze, incapable
Of piercing yet the mysteries involved ;
But now for ever lift, that all, who will,
May see those things, the mysteries reveal ;—
See the demands of law necessitous,
Now satisfied by one last sacrifice ;

And death and imperfection, both the work
Of evil, by perfection here disarmed ;
And hellish hate, invincible by aught,
Save heavenly love, now foiled and overthrown.
For evil in its darkest here is shown
By sacrifice, its self-wrought punishment,
The symbol still of that to which it leads,
Until frustrate by love, the source whence that
Provision springs, by which it is annulled,
By love, here in its highest now displayed,
An high example all may reverence ; for
Love is the ladder by which man ascends
Towards perfection and a higher life,
As hate is that by which he downward glides
To lower natures, tending unto death.

"And now, the great atonement made, behold
The Christ triumphant rises from the tomb
Despite the stone and seal official set,
And guard by Pilate to Caiaphas given ;
Joins His disciples and commissions them,
His word to preach and doctrine to make known
Unto all kindreds, tongues, Gentiles, and Jews,
Baptizing all, as many as are apt,

The word to hear, and fitted to receive,
That they thenceforth become one family,
Joined in the bonds of fellowship and love.
But He, His mission given, to heaven ascends,
Caught up in sight of all His followers,
Who thus assured of His Messiahship,
And ministry, beyond all shadow of doubt,
Go forth to teach, not fearful now, as once,
When they deserted Him, a prisoner led
To Caiaphas' hall and Pilate's judgment-seat ;
But full of life and energy the worst
To dare ; and in their sufferings rejoice,
Even to death, which they account the seal
Of their apostleship necessitous
Affixed, and proof of their high office, given,
That therein thenceforth all men may believe."

Thus passed before the Seraph in review,
And Traveller, as is here now summarised
With commentary annexed, the chief events,
That form on earth the history of mankind
During its early stage preparatory,
Under Mosaic, or hierarchal law.
Completed here, the primal system erst

Revealed, and the old order of things, long known
As types mysterious and symbols of that,
Which was, still is, and is to come, but now
Arrived in part, thence of their substance robbed
Proportional, must suffer change, and pass,
As now they pass, leaving the truths involved
In clearer light displayed, which while to some
Extent unto a chosen few made known,
Yet from the multitude were still concealed,
As things beyond their mental grasp, and all
Unsuited to the status of their age.
The rites they were enjoined to observe and con,
As children con their letters, not knowing why,
Or dimly seeing afar, to what they tend.
So likewise here, those types and ceremonies,
Now discontinued in th' observance, are
Henceforth as letters of an alphabet,
For by their aid we read, at least in part,
What otherwise we could not understand.

BOOK IV.

AFTER short pause the Herald spake and said :
"Prepare thee now to see in turn the new,
As thou hast seen the old order of things
Slowly arise and culminate and fall ;
The new, upon the old foundations raised,
Yet different else, shall grow, showing afar,
Like towering peak or mountain by the sea."

   Thence from a rocky eminence saw they then,
By power of Him, who in the present holds
The future and the past, a luminous cloud
Amid the darkness palpable, uprisen
As though it were a beacon in the night.
Upon a hill the silvery vapour lay,
A hill hard by, if not the Mount of Zion,
Within the compass of Jerusalem,
Whose frowning walls and towers impendent loomed,
Like shadows dim, athwart the lurid haze ;

Gigantic ruins that seemed to fade, withdrawn
Before that lucent cloud, which now increased,
Took form, assuming in the outline broad
The semblance of a mighty temple or hall,
With spires and domes and minarets adorned.
Besides more wonderful up-grew around,
Slowly evolved, whate'er of loveliness
Or beauty from the soul of nature drawn,
The outer sense can charm or touch the heart,
Remoulding it through sympathy divine :
Like sound of seas, all grandest harmony
Of voice and harp and organ breath combined,
In hymns and swelling anthems rolled on high ;
All sculptured forms of beauty, draped or nude,
Breathing of life, from snowy marble hewn,
Appealed to man and, eloquent, though mute,
Pointed the source whence they their beauty drew ;
And paintings still more exquisite *took* shape
Of angel, cherub, seraphim or saint,
Shedding sweet influence, melting, subduing
Or drawing the soul by love's attractive power.
The temple itself with worshippers was filled ;
Elders and priests innumerable thronged,
When lo ! a transformation strange appeared,

Slowly uprising in the midst, a Shape
Colossal towered, like shadow imminent,
That all the hierophants involved in gloom
And night disastrous on the people shed.
The Semblance wore the outward robes of peace ;
But divers passions lay, a motley crowd,
In every fold, and sowed the seeds profuse,
Of malice, envy, strife and rancorous hate ;
Pride, falsehood, sisters twin, outrage and wrong
And darkest tyranny went hand in hand,
Increasing still, till the impendent weight
Their downfall wrought. The forms of loveliness.
That erewhile shed their influence around,
Now seemed anomalous and out of place ;
And with the music, erst so heavenly,
The jarring squeak of blighted power uprose.
Dark superstition and dense ignorance,
Increasing still, prevailed, and denser grew,
Until the people, mutinous, combined ;
Gained strength therein, and warred against the Shape,
And overcame, wresting from him his power,
Which arrogated to themselves in turn,
New sects they form, new councils, codes, and rush
Into extremes ; each separate order, each

Of heresy, suspects ; and with the leaven
Of discord sown, maintains long time the strife.
But all seemed ordered so or fixed of Heaven,
That from the evil ever good accrued ;
For all contended so among themselves,
One counterbalancing the one, that each
The power of each, for evil neutralised ;
Whereby the baleful Tyranny was crushed,
Darkness dispelled and liberty regained :
True liberty increasing still, as light
Increasing, from the founts of knowledge risen,
The blinding clouds of ignorance dispelled,
Till lenience just, and charity became,
The custom of the hour, and tolerance
Intolerance and bigotry replaced.
Thus harmony returns : sectarian views
Confined, illiberal, expanded now,
No strife excite, nor longer stay the march
Of the broad principles of Christian faith ;
For this the faith uprisen, as here foreshown :
Persuasions, orders, sects, now reconciled,
All difference waive, approximating each,
In form, to each, for all one God adore,
One creed profess, one faith founded on love !

Where sat the Shape Briarean, like night
Dark'ning the land, now sits enthroned again
The saintly Forms of age, ven'rable age !
Mild, affable, breathing benevolence still
And love, that concord work and harmony.
Unfolding too, the mighty Temple soon
More glorious shone, and towering, met the clouds
And vaster still and higher seemed to grow,
Till slowly in the outline changed, the pile
Became anon a radiant city, square
On square, high wall'd and tower'd, wherein no church
Was found, temple, or sacrificial hall ;
Nor ever voice of prayer was heard ; for there
No sin, working deformity, had place,
For which by prayer or sacrifice to atone :
But ever rose instead the mighty swell
Of organ pipe with golden harp and voice
Of multitudes in song, loud as the rush
Of winds through norland pines, or torrent floods,
Thunder remote, or seas successive tossed
Tempestuous on the hollow-sounding shore !

Then passed the vision ; and his heavenly guide
The Traveller thus addressed. " Here hast thou seen

Before thee set, to what the worlds now tends ;
The means whereby this end is to be gained,
Or rather stage in circles infinite ;
For end, is none or rest, if rest be not
In endless perpetuity of change.
More nearly now the complicated wheels
Must thou discern, wherein revolve a time
The mysteries of life, the present phase
In chief thereof, and destiny of man,
Dimly revealed, disclosed as from afar."

He ceased ; and straight Jerusalem again
Uprose in view, showing, as previously
It showed ere in the luminous cloud removed,
And in the midst a body of men appear ;
Earnest they seem, and on th' accomplishment
Of some great object bent ; some mighty scheme
Of moment to the world, concerning which
In secret conclave they assemble oft,
Both laws to frame and officers to appoint
The work to press,—a work none other than
The reformation of a world, and change
From darkness into light ; a work enjoined
By Him of Nazareth : for followers those

Are of the Nazarene, on Calvary's hill
Late crucified, now risen from the dead,
The judge ordained and Saviour of mankind.
This, the foundation of that rising Church,
Of which these men the nucleus have formed,
And centre fixed ; from which emissaries
Are now being sent into the neighbouring towns,
Adherents there to seek and branches, form,
Till grown in strength, to distant lands they speed,
And climes, there too the work to carry out.
On every side 'gainst persecution they
Contend, nobly contend, and headway make ;
For they, by superhuman power upheld,
All opposition bring either to naught
Or to advantage turn ; till Churches soon
Established are in all the bordering states ;
Churches, that still unto Jerusalem, ·
As to their centre turn, and spiritual head ;
Turn yet awhile, until the time arrives,
Now near, that she shall under foot be trodden,
As on the Mount of Olivet foretold.—
O'erthrown in punishment, the just award.
Self-merited, of crime unparalleled ;—
O'erthrown, that in her overthrow alike,

Material evidence may therefrom accrue
As to the Word and the Messiahship
Of Him whom she reviled and crucified.

And lo ! already is the crisis come !
For, with the swift transition of a dream,
The phantom legions round Jerusalem close,
And then withdrawn a time, they see the saints
Afar remove, her judgments to avoid.
Portents and signs portending woes appear,
Omens and prodigies in earth and sky :
Sights supernatural, meteors and swords,
With fiery comets joined impendent hang,
Or o'er Jerusalem wave ; in air resounds
The din of war, and showers of blood descend ;
The temple gates, as if instinct with life,
Unbar themselves and on their hinges turn :
Sepulchral voices call, and grisly shapes,
Spectres and shrouded apparitions rise,
Confounding nature's rules to stalk at large,
As if the living and the dead were joined ;
And day and night a piercing cry alarms,—
A maniac's voice unutterably sad,
The tone itself, despair as of the grave,

And woe, the burden of its plaint,—woe ! woe !
Affrights the soul ;—woe to Jerusalem, woe !
Jerusalem where words of grace were heard,
Heard and rejected, now far other notes ;
Far other message borne, than words of love
Or hymns of peace by angel-choirs intoned.
Abrupt the Roman legions close again,
And on the air the din of battle swells ;
The rush of conflict, onset and repulse
And rallying charge alternately succeed ;
Death-dealing missiles fly, javelins and darts
With showers of stones from catapults propelled.
Huge battering engines thunder at the walls,
Hurling their beams against the rock-hewn tiers,
Till with a crash the riven ramparts fall.
Nor less inside the noise of battle storms ;
Each pause without but adds unto the rage
Of fighting factions penned within the gates.
There Simon, John, Eleazar, each 'gainst each,
Pitting their clans, for leadership contend :
Simon a time the upper city holds ;
And from the Temple, John expels the priest.
Revenge, hatred and rage relentless burn
As fire unquenchable within the breasts

F

Alike of all, the leaders and the led,
As though a band of furies 'mong them ran,
Fast urging them unto perdition's brink,
Like that swincherd in Galilee, possessed
Of Satan's imps, expelled from man to brutes,
Them to destroy, destruction still their bent.
Not all the sights of horror there disclosed
Their factious hate or vengeful ire can stay ;
The fellest forms of suffering there combined,
Calamities as from the fount of wrath,
Heart-rending agony, despair and death
And lunacy, pale famine and disease,
In them no fear, no sympathy excite.
The wounded, dead and dying swelter side
By side, as in one hideous lazar-house !
Cries, groans and execrations stun the sense ;
The dead, in heaps, are from the ramparts flung,
Exposed to-day ; yet fiercer swells the strife ;
For they with scorn all terms of peace reject ;
And by their shameless perfidy call down
More vengeance on their heads—call down, despite
The efforts and the will of him, who leads
The Roman Host, to save them from themselves.
Wall after wall is forced ; yet to the last

Offers of mercy are in turn held out,—
Held out, and urged by their own countryman,
Josephus, mouth-piece of the Roman power,
Commissioned, there, the word of Rome to plight,
And safety guarantee, if they desist.
But they, unto their ruin driven and doom,
All offers spurn, and acts of clemency
Repay in blood, that is repaid again
In equal meed, till men like demons fight.
Beams, roofs and battlements in wrath uptorn
Are on the Romans hurled : There Simon storms,
Leading his men ; and John speaks from the wall
Urging his followers to deeds of blood,
Wanton revenge and acts of cruelty,
Revenge rather than safety or defence !
Not Moloch in that pandemonium famed
Of spirits in Council met, spirits reprobate,
As fables tell, more violent than he,
Who now harangues, than John Gischala,
Or more upon his own destruction bent,
His own, insane, and that of all his tribe.
Still grows the storm, till, higher yet and higher,
The elements against Jerusalem fight
The fiery sword now shoots out tenfold flame ;

Fierce light'nings glare in dazzling sheets or forked
In ruin on the riven towers descend ;
Loud thunders peal, until the trembling earth
Commoved, responds with subterraneous roar ;
Unearthly moans and winds in tempest's voice
Resound afar, like dreary echoes heard
From desolate hall or haunted ruin's keep.

And now more wonderful the closing sign,
That marked the fate of Israel unfolds.
Hardly had night the zenith reached, when lo !
Around the Temple and the Holy Hill,
Where howled the wintry blast, thick clouds arise,
Pile heaped on pile, immovable as though
No breath the air had fanned, and all the mount
Straightway in darkness palpable enrobe.
Anon, as in a transformation strange,
A movement in the ebon mass appears :
The clouds, as by a light within revealed,
Compose themselves in form symmetrical
Of battlements and towers, dim, indistinct
Or shadowy at first, yet clearer showing,
As higher yet the airy building rose,
Until the pile, complete, stood forth to view,

An image of the Temple of Solomon,
Colossal 'mid the clouds of heaven upreared !
Within the sound of voices rose, a sound
Majestic and subduing, yet strangely sweet ;
A hymn that might have held the world in awe
Was heard ; for ne'er till then on human ears
Fell tone so solemn and sublime, so full
Of sadness, yet of grandeur and command !
" Let us go hence" was sang, " let us go hence !"
As from the mighty portal marched a host
" Such as man never saw before and such
As man shall never see but once again ;
The guardian angels of the city of David,
They came forth gloriously, but woe in all
Their steps, the stars upon their helmets dim
And tears down their celestial beauty flowing."*
" Let us go hence, let us go hence," they sang,
As yet upon the cloudy hill they stood.
" Let us go hence !" was heard magnificent
As on the air in light they rose sublime !
" Let us go hence !" resounded from afar !
Till with a crash the aerial battlements
Together rolled and on the wind dispersed.

* Salathiel's account of the fall of Jerusalem (Croly).

Lastly, the outworks passed and triple wall,
The Temple is assailed; the Holy House
And Sanctuary are to destruction doomed.
Here storming fury knows no bounds; nor aught
Avail the efforts of the Roman prince
The glorious pile to save ; the gates are forced,
The courts are fired and crackling flames ascend ;
Blood flows in streams ; and men like demons rage,
Or tigers, rather, of their whelps despoiled
And wounded sore, the spoilers in their midst.
Nor cease they, till the mighty walls and towers,
As in a furnace riven, with hideous fall
Descend, involving them in common ruin,
Gentile and Jew, one mingled holocaust,
One dreadful offering, immolated there,
Significant, in the great Temple of Law,
Law changeless and inexorable, still
Exacting th' utmost penalty, where aught
Defective under its operation comes.
But now for ever with its temple falls
The Nemesis of law, cast down at length
By that, which it in part exemplified
In sacrificial rites and outward forms
Of expiation through atoning blood ;

Meaning no less than imperfection changed
Unto perfection through the law of love.

So fell the Holy Temple, long the pride
Of Israel and the wonder of the world ;
The centre of that sacrificial type
Of worship, handed down traditional
In every clime : and with the temple fell
Jerusalem, built by Melchisedec,
And Salem called, and by the Jebusite
In later time, now level with the dust ;
Her walls and courts and palaces o'erthrown,
Her treasures sent the pomp of Rome to swell,
Her elders and her royal princes slain,
Her noble matrons, sons and daughters sold
To slavery and into exile driven,
And foreign lands, there separate to dwell,
A race despised, during revolving years ;
A standing witness to that light ordained
To guide mankind, and that new order of things
Through them uprisen, and based upon the old,
Or rather raised continuous thereon,
Another and a higher stairway set
In that great series, by which man ascends ;

For slowly, as from youth to age, doth man
Advance, gaining new light as he proceeds,—
Knowledge wherewith the power of evil here
To counteract, evolving good therefrom,
Until each grosser animal instinct,
Subdued or held in check by reason's curb,
Gives place proportional to higher thoughts,
And man towards the spiritual inclines,
Progressing still, until the climax reached
In this, he enters on another sphere ;
There too, as here, his upward way to find
Through cycles infinite or downward sink,
Seduced by evil, like those erring spirits
Who fell, reverting from their high estate.
But long shall be the struggle atween the good
And evil on these premises renewed.
The latter still essaying by fraud and force
And subtlety to thwart and countermine,
Or clad with argument, in reason's garb,
Vaunting expediency with shows of good,
Not good, self-righteousness the object sought ;
Self-righteousness complacently reviewing
Its meritorious acts, though prompted oft
With doubtful aim, and tinged with selfishness ;

But with vain sophistry excusing still
Each wordly lapse, or else condoning them
With hollow prayer, inefficacious breath,
Or worse, hypocrisy's first harbinger.
But good, relying on its innate power
Invincible, based on the sense of right
And heavenly truth, which is the substance, not
The show of things, useth no artifice
Or subterfuge but wisdom unalloyed,
That with simplicity still brings to nought
Or to advantage turns, against their aim,
The wiles of evil cunningly devised;
And unto violence and fear and hate
Opposeth naught but mildness, hope and love,—
Immortal love! the all-pervading Soul
Of nature, and the Eternal source of life
Prolific, and Creative Energy!
A vast discerning, sympathising power,
Ever essaying to draw unto itself
And from destruction save and loss, whatever
Of good within the grasp of evil lies.
For to destruction evil ever tends and death,
Descending by successive steps thereto,

Unless arrested in its downward course:
For such its function is, to wrest from good
By force or fraud, or injure and deform
Whate'er assailed or countermined may be;
And still, though foiled, to wage eternal war.
But hardly had the primal system fallen,
Or the old order its death wound had received,
Than westward sped the heralds of the new,
There in the home of Idolism upreared
On the elder faith, to burst the bonds of error
And break the spell of superstition's night.

Here spake the Seraph to his earthly Charge,
And said: "To westward now the rising flood
Of heavenly light doth flow, light without which
All knowledge were but pompous ignorance,
Leading to nought but foolishness and babble,
Or showing like taper in the midnight gloom,
Distorting vision while it helps to make
The dark around more palpable and drear.
Thither must we, and take our stand as now
Upon some hill or fitting eminence,
To view therefrom the current of events;

Or thence descend to mingle with the crowd
And nearer scan the complicated wheels,
The checks and self-adjusting balances,
That regulate, guide, hasten or retard
The checkered progress of Humanity.

BOOK V.

'TWAS night, and now her sister orbs shone out,
Watching in turn from their meridian heights
The slumbering earth in shadow laid and sleep,
When on an alpine range, in spirit clad
With mortal sense to heavenly pitch refined,
The Traveller found himself, uncertain how
He thither came, whether by sea or land
Or borne on air together with his guide.
A place they chose reclining by the brow
Of rude plateau commanding open view
Of mountain tract, ravine and hill and dale
And thence beyond unto the distant plains,
Now folded in the haziness of night.
Though high they stood, yet far above were seen
Those giant cones that rise abrupt and tower
Like Titans placed among the lesser hills.
Eternal snow or spirit in substance fixed,
Materialised from out the viewless ether,

By heaven's alchemic force, lay deep around,
Concealing there the nakedness of earth
And lending smoothness to the rugged slopes,
A bright perennial robe of spotless white
Disposed by winds in ever-shifting wreaths
Or fixed immovable in stony folds
And hollowed out fantastic into caves
And many chambered grots, ice palaces
With azure crystal gemmetl, the fair retreats
Of mountain Sprite or wandering Oread.
Upon the wide expanse of snow-clad hills
And seeming wastes a dreamy stillness lay,
A weird and solemn beauty dwelt around,
As though the Spirit of nature there had wrought
Her spells unseen beneath a canopy
Of circling clouds, where silvered by the moon
Upon the brow of neighbouring heights they stood.
A strange absorbing sense of mystery
Engrossed the faculties and filled the soul
With reverential awe, as though it felt
Instinctively that shadowy world were but
The mere projection, hull and instrument
Of kindred mind, and all the frozen waste
A promenade or intermediate home

Of spirit life ; nor felt the soul in vain ;
For light upon the air was heard the chime
Of instrumental touch and choral voice,
Faint, exquisite, and borne, as from afar,
Like silvery echo on the hollow breath
Of tumbling flood or cataract diffused,
Distinct, yet blending with the deeper tone,
Until anon it neared and louder grew
And louder still, till, rolling on the air
In floods of soul-dissolving harmony,
It swept through all the vast intricacies
Of sound, and palpitating, throbbed and leaped
And tossed like billows of an aerial sea,
Striking the spheres, till heaven's concave rang
With tumult of tempestuous symphony !
Then instantaneous burst upon the sight
A glorious vision of the world of spirit ;
For marshalled on the gilded clouds that lay
In piles, embanked upon the terraced hills
Or superficial spread from brow to brow
Aslant the vales, a thronging host appeared
In serried ranks of angel choristers ;
Spirits they seemed of either sex attired
In flowing robes with golden cinctures bound

And starred with gems ; Immortal beauty breathed
Ineffable, the common heritage
Of one and all, beauty in substance clad,
Substance ethereal deemed, yet substance still,
Not hollow show, but matter virtual,
The robe of spirit and the instrument,
Material yet imponderable ; for what
Is weight but a mere property, a mode
Of matter at the touch of spirit dissolved,
Retained or regulated by the will,
As likewise is solidity and form.
Thus on the clouds no empty pageant moved,
 But angels in ethereal substance robed,
In all their members tangible and real ;
Nor trod they there on barren clouds alone
Or wastes of snow illumined by the moon,
But rather now on azure fields bedecked
With flowers and radiant with a silvery glow,
Intense yet mellow as the light of even,
That streamer-like with splendours filled the air,
And flashing, shone unto the distant pole.
Such harmony and mingled loveliness
Transcendent played, absorbing soul and sense,
The Traveller cried, commoved to ecstacy

" Oh ! Guide let us for ever here remain !"
And smiling then, the Seraph thus replied.
" Wilt thou content thee with the lesser good,
Not seeing beyond, nor seek to reach a higher."
This saying, he bent on him his radiant eyes,
That with effulgence beaming shed new scope
Of vision on his soul ; then further spake,
" Now look and tell me wilt thou here remain ?"
He looked and found his mortal sight was changed.
Space now no obstacle presents, the view
To dim, as heretofore, contracting it
To earthly span ; the planetary worlds
Around him wheel, and suns and systems rush
Upon his sight, no longer as stars remote
Or glimmering points in dim perspective lost ;
But countless and immeasurable orbs
In their appalling distances revealed
Interminable throughout th' infinitudes
Of endless space, till vision failed to pierce
The deep immensity and glancing thought
In presence of the Infinite recoiled.
Sun rose on sun, as on they sped, and world
On world, majestic in their orbits poised,
Sweeping through space incomprehensible,

Where all now seemed above or all below,
For height was lost in depth, abysmal tracts
Where billowy systems rolled in concert round
Some mighty pole, and on the boundary seemed
Of death and night, till other systems shone,
Beyond the vast vacuities revealed ;
And others still, nor ever came an end
Until the Traveller cried, oppressed in soul,
"Oh Angel give me back my mortal sight !
My spirit aches with this infinity !
O'erwhelming is the glory here displayed
Insufferably grand beyond all thought !
Rather let me with earthly things abide,
Or change this human heart, to earth attuned,
This heart that weeps, and fears and fondly hopes"*
" Nor hopes in vain," the Seraph straight replied,
" Such change shall be the work of time or else,
Indeed, this vision were not granted thee.
Now rest, for with this lower world as yet
Awhile thou hast to do." So saying, in sleep
His eyes he sealed, but softly in his ears
The sound of choral music murmuring played,
Soothing the sense and mingling with the soul !

* See " *Orbs of Heaven,*" page 195.

G

So slumbered he in blissful calm, nor woke
Till morn, first glancing on the icy cones,
Repelled the dark and set hills aglow
With mimic flame and high uprolled the mists
That shroud-like lay on river and lake and dell
Till painted in the purple heavens they hung,
Or, shrinking else, in viewless air dissolved.

Before them now in ample prospect lay
Wide upland tracts, composed irregular
Of hill and dale, with primal forests laden ;
And thence beyond, vast undulating plains,
Broad lands with flocks and lowing herds besprent,
Extended to the far horizon's bound
Or to the sea. Towns, villages were seen,
Thick clustering or at intervals disposed,
And cities walled, nor fell the vision short
Of Tiber's flood, where mighty Rome in state
Sat on her seven hills, queen of the earth ;
And proudly sat, and worthily, the work
Magnificent of human genius sprung ;—
Genius of gods or of the gods inspired,
Far reaching, free, untrammelled, unconfined !
As testified in magnitude of scale,

In vast display and the completeness met
In every part of the stupendous whole.
Parks, gardens, avenues and templed groves
With grots and founts and terraces adorned,
Replete besides with snow-white statuary
In single form or group heroic cut
Or fashioned else in beauty's softer mould;
And baths and aqueducts and theatres,
Temples, triumphal arcs and citadels,
Patrician halls and regal palaces,
The home of kings or more than kings declare
The wealth, the genius and magnificence
Of earth's metropolis, Imperial Rome,
Now at her height and hastening to her fall,
Degen'rate grown, her kindling genius lost
Through irreligion, selfishness and crime.
Her fostering deities, so potent once,
Now names become, inanities unfeared
Or, worse, as gods through fashion still upheld
And with false breath in mockery adored;
Yet unbelieved, thence powerful for evil,
A show not substance, or vain ritual
By which, truth in hypocrisy is merged,
To the subversion of the intellect.

Such Rome was now or such her habitants;
Her old religion fallen, a new uprisen,
But not yet in the vacant place installed :
Nor easily, where priestly power, alarmed,
And tyranny their ancient weapons wield
Of force and fear, blind superstition's tools;
Self-interested, trying in vain to stay
The march of truth, of light and liberty.
Hence Rome a sea of horror now presents
Unparalleled, where tyrants wade in gore,
Like blinded demons in destruction's whirl
Fiercely destroying, till in the torrent drowned,
And truth prevailed, uprising on the flood !
Uprising too more vigorous and bright,
Henceforth incapable of suffering harm
From outward force or enemy declared.
Yet hardly is the fierce oppression ceased,
When lo ! excluded from without, the spirit
Of evil essays, with wily art disguised,
To reach the source and taint the fount of light ;
But finding it incapable of stain,
Around it piles a superincumbent mass
Of broken fragments from the ruins culled
Of Pagan creeds and dying Hellenism,

Wherewith to hide it from the people's gaze,
Till it be made a source of evil in turn,
A tool of tyrants and oppressors still
As terrible as those it once removed.

Soon persons, places and observances
Of outward forms replace the spirit of truth,
And ceremonies and modes of worship, deemed
More efficacious and restorative
Than unimpeached sincerity of heart
And more acceptable in sight of Heaven.
Thence prayers or journey made to shrine of saint,
Jerusalem or the tomb on Calvary,
Are more important held than works of love,
And of themselves sufficient thought to absolve
From sin and reparation make in full
For every deed of treachery and blood.
And hence a gradually increasing throng,
By vows constrained, unto Jerusalem turn,
A motley crowd of pilgrims first unarmed
And peaceably inclined, till harshly used,
They grow indignant of the wrongs enforced :
And thence returning to their native homes
Stir up a crusade 'gainst the Infidel.

Then fired with zeal a banded host advance,
Who wrest Jerusalem from the Moslem power,
And for a time with varied fortune hold
The sovereignty, till growing corrupt,
Factious and false, a nuisance in the land,
They are by the great Saracen expelled;
The Saracen more worthy of command,
The foe avowed of falsehood and deceit,
Whose word inviolate, was sacred held,—
A soldier proved, wise temperate and humane,
A Christian, though an Islamite in faith;
He in good truth, they only in pretence.
But who, in their presumption deemed that Heaven
Cared more for creeds than singleness of heart.
Nor less in Rome did vanity and pride
And love of power and grasping avarice
Religion and all sacred truths degrade
To worldly ends, till they mere merchandise
Became, and levers in the hand of power,
Gold to extort or influence to hold.
Dense ignorance, stagnation and decay
In spiritual and temporal things result.
The once Imperial City from whence spread,
Flowing as from a central reservoir,

To lands remote or sunk in barbarism,
A tide of civilisation and the laws
Of government, cohesion and the arts
Of cultured life, is now become a waste
Of mounds and mouldering ruins, heaped and piled,
Proud monuments of heaven-born genius once !
Genius long silent, yet here living still
Through these dark centuries to kindle anew
The flame divine when dawning doth appear.
Sad, solemn and impressive now they stand
In dim and weird sublimity, instilling
The secrets of their origin and fall,
And former history, until such time
As they shall find, more fully understood,
A voice in man to second or expound,
What they so forcibly in silence moved :—
In silence, till the dawn, so long delayed,
Now come, a mighty voice responds, as though
To ruin, it were in sympathy attuned :—
A world-wide wail of sorrow infinite
In mystic and unfathomable song,
A chilling wail heartrending and undying
Of fierce regret and ever-gnawing pain
And misery begotten of the past,

Th' award of time misspent, the heritage
And sad result of lives of perfidy,
Called to account and judged of nature's law.
Nor is their spell and kindling influence
Confined, incentive unto song alone ;
Lo ! 'mid those ruins and the wrecks of art
What Titans intellectual rise, upcalled
At length, true scions of the mighty dead !
Titans whose every burning thought is form
Whose touch is life, embodied life expressed
In Beauty and in Symmetry divine !

'Twas thus before the Traveller and his guide
The strife of centuries passed ; nor came an end
As though it were a law necessitous
Imposed, that good through evil must advance ;
The good sublimed and tested in the trial,
The evil o'erthrown, its punishment entailed,
Wherein, it is its own appointed scourge
And, like a scorpion, stings itself to death ;
Yet soon revives, the combat to renew.
For there, no sooner had the new belief
Become the paramount religion than
New heresies arise, permitted still,

As if in punishment ordained of those,
Who, while they may, will not accept the light,
Preferring darkness rather ; or inclined
To evil, seeing, would pervert the truth
Entrusted to their charge, and lower fall,
Bringing a worse destruction on themselves.
Hence found unfitted to receive the light
Unto delusions are delivered up,
And fancies crude, yet more in mercy than
In punishment, for thereby are they saved
The harder lot, the greater crime involves,—
The greater crime, in that they would reject
The proffered truth, beholding it unveiled,
Untempered or unsuited to their sight,
Accustomed only to the twilight haze :
But veiled, as now, in part it is discerned,
And thence, the more, accepted in good faith
A power for good proportional becomes.
For, although dimmed, its essence is unchanged ;
And not the less can those, who will, discern
In higher degree its innate loveliness,
By wisdom led or by that surer light,
That faculty implanted in the soul,
To cleave the veil, as lightning cleaves the dark,

Our reason's guide that of itself alone
Presumptuous or incredulous would stray,
Spinning the brittle clue or argument,
Till lost in endless labyrinths of doubt :
But aided thus, a helper it becomes,
A mental power that in the exercise
New vigour and a wider scope attains ;
For here it is a law of Heaven ordained,
That man through effort shall advance himself.

Thus was the truth, though veiled by man's device,
Still visible to those who could discern ;
Yet to the multitude as darkness was,
Or darkness seen by dubitable light,
In that from view it was in part withdrawn ;
And, so withdrawn, was made itself in turn
A pretext in the hand of tyranny,
A hind'rance, and the direst implement
Of horror in fell superstition's grasp.
For in the sacred name of truth profaned,
Embodied falsehood, still the foremost stay
Of evil, enacted now its darkest deeds
Of blood, of outrage, violence and force ;
Enacted boldly in the sight of heaven,

Nor feared in aught the consequence thereof ;
For superstition like a nightmare sat
Grim, threatening on the nation's heart to curb
Every attempt or motion at redress.
So evil prospered in the garb of truth,
Till overgrown, then loss sustained therefrom,
And rents, through which the light concealed within,
Disclosed at times, the nature of the mask ;
And so disclosed, some leaders of the realm
With bolder mien, from clear sight endowed,
Sought to release the multitude, enslaved,
Who, long oppressed, were now not indisposed
To 'scape from darkness and embrace the truth ;
For straightway from being led, leaders themselves
In turn became, and champions of the light,
Together bound, determined to achieve
Their liberty and superstition quell
Within its hold or perish in th' attempt.
Unequal though at first the contest seemed,
Yet perseverance in the cause of truth
And firm resolve not to submit or yield
However tried or worsted in the strife,
Eventually to victory attained ;
And evil fell, fell of necessity,

Its overgrowth, here hastening its o'erthrow.

Yet truth no less a signal victory won ;

But evil, though thus checked, again revives,

In other shape, its mission to fulfil :

Revives, not now on central seat upraised,

A mighty shadow towering to the sky,

But humbler, though not less inveterate,

Essays to gain in divers lands and realms

What of its old ascendancy it lost ;

And to that end begins by sowing anew

The seeds of enmity and hate undying

Atween the falling and the rising faith,

And 'tween the divers sects themselves now risen

In consequence of liberty proclaimed,

And freedom in all matters of belief.

Sectarian hate and prejudice ensue :

Though humble at first, each rival sect anon,

Gaining th' ascendancy, the tyrant plays,

Its violence within due bounds restrained

Rather by law, than aught of tolerance

On equity or sense of justice framed.

Yet irrespective of the evil wrought

By persecution and the abuse of power,

Much good ensues ; for in the rivalry

A healthy stimulus to zeal is found,
Besides a stay 'gainst indolent routine
So oft the herald of hypocrisy
And self-deceiving pharisaic prayer,
A long harangue of words irrelevant
Availing nought or worse injurious found.
But balancing the evil with the good,
True liberty by rivalry obtained
Outweighs the whole and of itself repays
For all the disadvantages entailed,
The outcome of sectarian prejudice.
For with true liberty fair Science rose,
Advancing queenly with majestic mien
Strife and sectarian tyranny to allay,
And rear her throne on superstition's wreck.
Fair Science, lifting high her stately head,
With truth all radiant, comes now to unfold
To Man the mysteries of the universe,
And to him impart the secrets of her power,
That he too may the elements constrain
To do him service, as of right, his thralls
Made o'er to him, if he observe with care
The terms of contract and conditions fixed,
As in the book of nature's law laid down.

Instructed thus the human race attains
A civilisation far advanced, and state
Beyond the limits of what possible
Was held or deemed or hitherto conceived ;
A civilisation of itself a sign
Of that subjection of the world, to man
Committed, in that primal order given,
" Go forth, replenish and all earth subdue,"
A feat approaching its accomplishment,
Which, when achieved, will mark th' allotted term
Of man's career of self-development,
And trial in his present state, here, closed,
What time, he enters on another phase,
Another round of destiny to complete.

Meanwhile all selfish bickerings subside ;
And sects, now concious of their own defects,
Of others much more tolerant become ;
And, rivals only in good works, prefer,
All unto all, the hands of fellowship
In love to extend and Christian brotherhood ;
And waving difference, in one cause, as one
Unite against the common enemy.

Thus harmony ensues : Religion now,
In principle and practice reconciled,
No empty name or hollow show is found ;
But with the spirit of charity imbued
Becomes, as erst, a vital power once more,
A humanising element through which,
Humanity a higher level gains.
But straightway evil, not to be outdone,
Th' assault renews by other plans, with skill
Devised, such progress to subvert or stay,
Or at the least, retard and neutralize
What otherwise may not be overcome.
And to this end, a gen'ral apathy
Is first induced in matters of belief :
Professions and outward conformity
Suffice the multitude, now careless grown,
Mere followers of ceremonial show
Or wordy forms at intervals rehearsed,
Like parrot phrases, signifying naught.
Religion suffers to a like degree,
Failing according to its hollowness
Until at length, distrustful of its mission,
And at th' advance of unbelief alarmed,
It back recoils and from the contact shrinks

Helpless, unable of itself to oppose
Aught with effect, the inroad to resist ;
Till at th' advantage taken, Scepticism,
With the pretended might of science armed,
Essays in turn to drive her from her seat,
Though she likewise the aid of science claims,
Or humbly rather in distraction begs ;
For each would fain have science their ally ;
But Science, scorning hollowness and shift,
Holds on the even tenor of her flight,
Nor either helps, till in her own good time,
Swift as a falcon stooping from the clouds,
A writhing snake hooked fast either claw,
To heaven ascends and dashes them to earth,
Mangled and stunned, she, rising in her might,
Not otherwise shall seize and downward hurl
The hollowness of both, the patched-up forms
Of sect, obstructive and incongruous,
The rhetoric and imbecile displays,
Oracular deemed of dim-eyed Atheism,
That like the owl with vision circumscribed
To narrow nightly range, grows garrulous
On every trifle picked up in the dark.

Meanwhile with keen and unabating zeal
The subtle agencies at work essay
To sap the base of civilisation's tower,
And with it hurl from its high pinnacle,
So hardly scaled, Humanity itself.
Even now it seems to totter imminent,
A mighty ruin, to its centre mined,
And charged throughout with dark explosive fire.
Around it tempests rave ; conflicting waves
Uprolled, advance as on abysmal deeps,
Converging with destruction fraught and doom,
Until encountering with resistless shock,
Each whelmeth each, and mingling, passeth on ;
And mightier grows, still adding to its mass,
Till swollen beyond the bounds assigned, it parts
With force, and like a shattered mountain falls.

And now they were aware that in the West
And East alike, such tempest waves had risen,
Surcharged with fierce exterminating wrath,
And threat'ning, bore right down upon each other.
The Eastern tide advancing mightier seemed,
Its might not of itself original sprung,
But of the West designedly obtained

In preparation of the coming strife.
Yet all invincible and more compact,
The West advancing, like a deluge swept
Resistless on, whelming all obstacles
Beneath its flood : The elements, commoved
To sympathy, in opposition raged,
And globes of fire and fiery meteors burned
Or stream-like shot along the lurid sky ;
And ominous signs and apparations dire
And boding cries the souls of men alarmed.
The trembling earth responding heaved and moaned,
As though she felt an inward agony.
But clouds of sulphureous steam now gathering, soon
In darkness undistinguishable hid
The wild commotion and the rage alike
Of storming elements and nations met,
In conflict fierce, to drain the cup of wrath,
The measure full, of foul corruption brewed :
Thence unto judgment thus delivered up
And so adjudged from nature's awful code,
That they, themselves their judgments shall work out.

But straightway here, the Angel spake and said :
" Let this suffice, this outline briefly shown,

Of what shall yet in latter days befall ;
For further is not given thee to know.
So let us hence, and see what states precede
The advent of these judgments imminent."

BOOK VI.

Now rapidly as in a dream they sped
Where lay irregular a table-land,
In width of circle, bounded by the sea ;
And towards the side a mighty mountain rose,
And congregated on its slopes were seen
Innumerous crowds, of many peoples formed.
Arranged in zones at different altitudes,
Each took their stand, yet not to these confined ;
For many to the zones above made way
By slow degrees and unremitting toil.
And many still in circles journeyed round
And round the mount, and neither rose nor fell.
Others descended, though they knew it not,
Nor cared to know, but still the way pursued,
That lay before, indifferent where it led.
A shrouding mist and blinding fogs around
The basement hung, where many disappeared.
But on the middle and the upper slopes
No cloud remained, but still the light increased,

Till round the top a dazzling radiance shone.
Yet none within the upper zone might come
Or rest upon the top, save One that seemed
Greater than human, yet of human mould,
Who statue-like, high elevated stands
Alone upon the summit, pointing still,
With all the dignity of conscious power,
To other states in other worlds beyond :—
Stands unapproached, the Pre-ordained of Heaven,
In whom the Archetype is realized,
In whom the Image of the Deity
On man conferred, is in its highest evolved,
As needs it should, ere man perfection gained.
Likest to Him in form and countenance
Are they who stand immediately below,
And who with wonder ever and delight
Behold Him in unclouded majesty.
And next come those upon the middle zones,
Who see Him, yet not clearly as they ought.
But least like Him, of all upon the mount,
Are they, the tribes that wander round the base.
Nor wonderful, since nought of Him they know,
Or if they know, know only by report,
Not seeing Him, so far above them placed.

Yet most diversity was still observed
Among the dwellers midway on the slopes,
Who differ from each other in degree,
According to the measure of their sight;
For some ascend, and some retain their place
Upon the hill, while many downwards fall.

But now 'twas manifest, that to correct
The indistinctness of their vision due
To distance, that the latter had recourse
Unto a plan with skill devised and care
To meet their needs and difficulties remove.
Each different group or section has procured
A fitting likeness of the Archetype
Or Primal Form high placed upon the mount,
Whom henceforth chiefly in the abstract they
Shall contemplate according to their light,
Whilst holding still as matter of belief
The real existence of those qualities,
Now in the likeness easier expressed.
And thence assembling round the effigy,*
Exalted high, in royal robes attired,

---

* The effigies have reference to the different forms of Christianity embodied in the different modes of worship, which modes also constitute the robes or vesture of that form, and do not refer singly to any particular denomination.

They join in rites and ceremonial shows
Decreed in honour of th' Original,
Who, in the abstract, hard to realize,
Is in the concrete sought to be revealed.
Nor was the plan a failure or devoid
Of merit, so long as in the abstract they,
As in a glass, the Archetype beheld.
But on the concrete growing more intent
Many from the Original withdraw,
Deceived by show or led by indolence
To contemplate the effigy alone.
Till they, imagining that they ascend,
Unwittingly to lower circles fall.
For lo ! instead the effigy they think
The same, unchanged, they venerate a mask
In counterfeit by Evil now prepared
Unknown to them and hoisted in its place,
That they, thereby, like injury may sustain
And come to be like that which they revere.
Such was in part, the worship thus observed,
And in effect such was its tendency.

But here the Traveller and his Guide came nigh,
Or rather joined the concourse on the mount,

Now jubilant in full assembly met,
As was the custom 'fore the effigy,
When lo ! a strange occurrence was observed ;
For from among them one that bore the sign
Of innate power, with confidence advanced,
And to a grove sequestered and apart,
Betook him where a snow-white statue stood,
A statue of a woman in her prime
Attired in flowing drapery, that robed
But did not hide her symmetry of form,
And by her side a child, or more than child,
Fair as a cherub in majesty reclined.
He came and touched the statue, and a thrill
Of life shot through the marble limbs and lit
The countenance and flashed within their eyes,
And bounding, coursed the channels of the soul.
Instinct with life the marble forms descend,
Each from its place, obedient to the will,
And hand in hand accompany their guide,
Who now returning, led them whence he came,
And set them midst th' assembled multitude,
That here fell back in blank astonishment.
And then, unmindful of the crowd agape
With wonder, went unto the effigy,

And from its features rent the mask and tore
The robes therewith that long from sight concealed
A complex form of foul monstrosity;
For divers shapes within the outer lay,
Transparent each and in their several shades
In order of a strange gradation ranged.
Degenerate types of human form are seen,
Misshapen, meagre, crooked or angular;
Nor are the types to human forms confined,
But orders of a lower class appear;
Inferior tribes in serial rank arranged,
Till in the midst a loathsome serpent lay.
Then turning to the multitude he said,
" Lo ! what you worship, that you shall become !
How like you this ! is it an image of Him
Upon the mount, or is it what you see ?
A monster which your drapery concealed.
Know you, that like the breathing marble there,
Pure, homogeneous and of human mould,
Single, symmetrical and undisguised
In all their parts your effigies must be."

Here wondering asked the Traveller of his Guide,
" What means the strange gradation thus unveiled

Of complex forms within the effigy ?"
And in reply the Seraph spake and said.
" Look and examine well that table-land
Below the mount, for there the answer lies."

And now they saw, that from the mountain-side,
Emerging from the mist, a chain of hills
Extended far upon the plain and passed
Into a desolate waste of rocks, that like
The ruins of a shattered mountain seemed.
And many from the upper circles now
Traverse the ridge, for one advanced before,
Has marked the course, untrod till then or known,
And on the heights an easy roadway formed.
Around the range of lesser hills are grouped
The lower tribes according to their rank,
Through kingdom, class, order and family,
Extending down till lost upon the plain.
But of the higher, arranged upon the hills,
Though to their orders fixed immutable,
A well-marked series of successive steps
Occurs each seeming in itself distinct
And separate, yet pointing in its turn
To steps above or grades below it placed.

Along the hills, extending from the mount
Right on unto the gloomy rocks beyond,
That rise abrupt in broken fragments piled,
The series in this fashion is maintained.
But on the mount and on the range of hills
All grades of being, however different
Or seemingly in outer form unlike,
Are based upon a common type or plan,
Though modified to meet the wants of each ;
Diversity in conformation still
Increasing as the scale of being ascends,
Till, in the higher, its limit is attained.
Thus by successive steps the groups advance
From lower forms to higher and more complex :
Then stationary remain, a time unchanged,
Till changed conditions draw them from the scene,
And nature calls up others in their stead.
But conversely, and on a smaller scale,
Receding or descending grades appear ;
For near the limit of the range of hills,
Among th' outlying spurs. and placed beside
The broken rocks, though not in line direct
Between them and the hills with which they join,
But towards the left, a gloomy vale deep lies.

And in the vale, descending from the spurs,
From higher orders of their class declined,
Is found the Serpent or Ophidian tribe,
Degraded, vilest of all living forms
On Vertebrate or Spinal system framed :
Degraded, but yet based upon the type
That on the range and Human mount prevails.
Degraded, loathsome, venomous and prone,
Lowest of creatures, on their bellies placed,
Deprived of outward or divergent limbs,
And on the ground for ever doomed to crawl
With tortuous motion, gliding on their ribs,
And forced to swallow still the dust that clings
Unto the slime bedaubed foul on their prey.
Within the upper portions of the vale
The lesser grades innumerable abound,
Whose deadly powers lie in their poison fangs ;
But towards the middle and the lower reach
Dragons of sorts more terrible abide,
Of length enormous and increasing size,
Till quitting land they vanish in the sea.
But it was seen that though the Serpent's vale
Ran from the hills, yet by a winding ridge
It was more with the rocky waste conjoined

Than with the hills, though they, likewise, from
    thence
Their origin derived, though more direct,
By ridges on a higher level placed,
Than that which to the Serpent's valley wound.
For here it was apparent that the hills
Had altogether in the waste arisen,
And from it were prolonged ; and that the waste
Was but the ruins of former hills that were ;
For all about uncouth remains were found,
Huge wrecks of life and relics of the past,
Strange fossil bones, in fragments or entire,
And skeletons, of size tremendous, piled
Among the rocks or bedded in the soil :—
Colossal and unwieldy forms preserved
In stony trance through ages fabulous,
As though the aim and purpose of their being
Were incomplete and yet to be wrought out,
Or being wrought in some mysterious way ;
For though entranced they seem to live still on,
And wait a call to active life once more.
Nor seem in vain, for lo ! one from the mount
Among them moves, and with a magic wand
Arouses them, as from unconscious sleep.

Earth trembles and the quaking rocks become
As liquid air or fleecy clouds embanked ;
And pervious now, an easy passage yield—
The mighty bones upstarting seek their kin,
And disencumbered of their shrouds unite—
Each in its place, and take their wonted forms,
And clad in flesh, their previous lives resume ;
For all is changed ; no longer rocks appear,
But stately trees and vast primeval woods,
And misty seas and rank and steaming plains
And lakes and rivers, estuaries and fens,
Where divers monsters bellow, chafe and war
And roam and browse or in their armour bask,
Or seek their prey, or flap on sounding wings
Like demons or like harpies in the night.
Then all again as in a dream grew vague ;
Plains, rivers, mountains, woods and primal seas
Revert and pass, each fusing into each,
Or changing place, new combinations form,
To change in turn ; for many on the mount
Hold distant conversation and discuss
With others here, now from the mountain come ;
And by their several spells, in concert wrought,
The history of our former world disclose,

Developing, though indistinct, each phase
And change concomitant as they occurred
In outline or in relative extent
Of land and sea and habitable earth,
With all the grades of life that appertained,
Whether of plant or animal, annexed
Until the whole scene upon scene uprose
Successively and interfusing passed,
And nought remained but barren rocks once more.

But here the mount itself and range of hills
Grew indistinct and were in mist involved.
And passing thence, escorted by his Guide,
The Traveller came unto a place remote,
A valley from the Serpent's vale derived
Or from it by a narrow gorge prolonged
Among the rocks, inclining to the right,
Until it passed into a dismal realm,
A land of sorrow and perpetual gloom,
Where all things in a hazy light appeared ;
Where fens and pools and inky waters lay
And lapped 'mong caves or washed upon the shore ;
And Titan woods all dark and silent stood
Or moaned, by melancholy winds disturbed.

And 'mong the woods and 'mong the rocks and caves
And by the margin of the gloomy flood,
Vast shadows throng, and shapes of divers mould
Pass and re-pass with sullen step or stand
All huge and gaunt in ghostly attitude,
Like skeletons of wasting famine wrought ;
Each to their habitats in this dim vale
Assigned and limited, as erewhile they,
In primal woods by lakes and fens, had been.
And 'mong them, unconfined and free to range
Through each domain, are shadows as of men,
Earth's aborigines, uncultured, fierce,
Of mighty bone, unclothed or clad in skins.
And by the caves and chiefly by the tide,
With axe and club, the restless phantoms flee
Or wander by, as though they looked for food
Or sought to trap or get the game in view.

But lying further on beyond the caves,
Without the woods and by the dismal shore,
Like broken rocks in shapeless fragments piled
The ruins, as of an ancient city spread
All desolate ; and towards the western side,
A mighty pile, high towering like a mount,

Embattled round and fenced with jutting stone,
Stands close upon the borders of the flood.
Unclosed by gates, the broken arches frown,
Like cavern mouths beneath a mountain's brow ;
And from them stairs and gloomy passages
Ascend the galleries, traverse the halls,
And wind afar unto the central courts,
That lie unroofed and open to the sky.
And in the distance lesser ruins stand
With tarns between and moors and blasted trees,
That, ghostlike in the dim uncertain light,
Their giant trunks and naked arms upraise.
And by each chamber, passage, nook and keep,
In blood-stained dress or tattered robes attired,
Unkempt and pallid spectres slowly glide
Or fly alarmed with wild sepulchral shriek,
Or sweep disorderly with rushing sounds,
Like those of whirlwinds and of thunders joined,
Or chariots on a hollow roadway rolled ;
Or lonely sit in damp and mouldering halls
Silent and sad, each countenace impressed
With deepest woe, but bearing still the signs
Of passion and the marks in life acquired,
Of hate and pride and malice and deceit,

I

In punishment, returned upon themselves,
Their own tormentors for the time, as doomed,
They sit or flee in these dim halls confined :—
In halls where silence is unbroken, save
By winds without, and waters and the rush
Of shades heard nightly with the fearful cries
Of anguish and the sobbings of remorse !

But here the Man, with sadness overcome
And heart sick melancholy at the sight
Of so much sorrow, wretchedness and pain,
Now asked his Guide what might the ending be,
What hope existed of respite or change,
In ages hence, to misery so great.

Then thoughtfully the Seraph spake and said.
" Thou knowest thyself, for it has been revealed,
This punishment is fairly meted out,
And neither more nor less than that which they,
Themselves accumulated and laid up,
The fruit of desolations wrought on earth
And evils dealt upon their fellow-beings ;
The breaking of the ties of life and love
And happiness on narrow selfish grounds,

Or like King Ahab by evil spirits deceived,
Or urged by envy, hatred and revenge,
Regardless of the wrongs of blighted hope
And of the sad and longing life of woe
On others forced in dungeons, or at large,
For friends in durance, or of life bereaved ;
Yet vainly hoped on Heaven to impose,
Unmindful or despite of nature's law,
And pardon win by prayer, repentance feigned,
And mummery, imposing on themselves ;
Here undeceived, for all in substance bear
The history of their former lives revealed.
Yet none of these unto those grounds confined,
Are wholly bad or of all good devoid.
Hence their contrition, sorrow, and regret,
The signs of higher nature still unquenched,
And of the good that yet within them lives :
And which in time shall their redemption work,
And transference from this to other states.
For although evil ever tends to death,
Where unopposed, and in extinction ends,
It seems a portion of the scheme of life,
The appanage and complement of good ;
And without which, the good could not exist
Or in its highest ever be evolved.

" But let us hence and see what yet remains.
There is a place hard by those dusky rocks
That vaguely rise into the lurid air,
Where thou shalt see in stages ultimate
The foul deformities of evil wrought,
And unto death consigned ; or such of them
As with impunity thou canst behold."

And passing thence beyond the rocks they came
Unto the entrance of a dismal gorge
That yawned beneath a frowning precipice,
And led into a chambered mount or hill
Or what seemed such, for it was hollowed out
And fashioned into vast and gloomy vaults
And courts, that lay 'mong rows irregular
Of shapeless stone or huge basaltic rocks,
And winding ran, from outer air removed,
Into the dim recesses of the hill.

But here, like one who suddenly recoils,
Alarmed in presence of some fearful thing,
The Man drew back, for far within were seen
Distorted shapes and foul monstrosities
And complex dragon-forms descending still

To lower grades, till in extinction lost.
But those of human shape compounded stood
Apart, and in their hideous ghastliness
Of form and feature far outdone and passed
The grades of animal monstrosity,
Though they, likewise stage after stage, appeared
To sink thereto and lose their human form.
And as they sink, become less hideous, for
They lose therewith their dread malignity,
Proportional, and diabolic power,
That unto fiends in human shape belong;
For fiends they are and ministers of evil,
By hatred rage and enmity impelled,
Whose only peace in dire destruction lies.

But to the Man, who trembling now stood by,
A flash within of lurid light revealed
Their hideousness in part, and only in part,
For he, about to fall, of sense deprived
At sight so dire, was like a child removed
Hence by his Guide, who gently tended him
Till consciousness returned; then to him said,
" What of the Evil in its substance now,
Thou hast beheld, whether, in downward course,

By grades, unto annihilation doomed,
Or midway in its progress stayed and foiled
By Good, as in the gloomy halls revealed.
Was on the mount collectively pourtrayed
By complex forms within the effigy;
Each within each, monstrosities more dire
Than Circe's cup or Momus' spells e'er wrought.
But on the fellest grades of evil here
In human form, thou couldst not look and live;
For as that form within itself combines
Perfection absolute, of love wrought out,
And therefore the embodiment in full
Of highest beauty, grace and symmetry,
So likewise in that shape debased and fallen,
Are grades of ghastly ugliness expressed.
And foul deformities of hate produced
So terrible that man may not behold;
For spirits of evil in their fellest forms
Are like the Gorgon's head with serpents twined,
Th' award of Pallas to Medusa given,
That turned to stone whoever looked thereon;
And, severed by the hand of Perseus, then
On Libyan sands a serpent brood produced.
So they, till of the human shape deprived

By Heaven's decree, are ministers of death ;
Less potent when to serpent forms constrained ;
To serpent forms, wherein their deadly hate
Is still expressed, but not their fatal power.
So Heaven wills, for in the Dragon shape
The lowest stage of evil is pourtrayed ;
The stage to which from higher grades it fell,
The change within itself of nature wrought ;
Its deadly hate, deceit and cunning still
Expressed in full, but unto weakness joined ;
For now, of outward limbs deprived and shorn,
It is perforce unto the earth confined ;
There doomed to crawl ; its sole remaining power
In sinuous fold or poison fang retained.

　　Such was the purport of the dream that so
Perplexed thee, which thou couldst not understand ;
That vision of the group at enmity,
The Evil One that warred against the man
And woman, and by fraud o'ercame and held
The mastery, till by the Child subdued.
And hence the meaning of that elder speech ;
" Since thou hast done this thing thou art henceforth
Above all creatures curst ; dust shalt thou eat

And prostrate on thy belly shalt thou go,
And I, between thee and the woman's seed,
Will enmity undying put ; His heel
Thou shalt contuse, but He shall bruise thy head."

" But thou hast seen that though the evil falls,
Before the good and to extinction tends,
Yet from it still a stream of life doth flow,
For it is part the universal scheme,
That highest good through effort is attained.
And such the teaching of that sacred Word
To man revealed, that guided by the same,
And by the light of truth and reason led,
He may o'er evil the mastery obtain,
And still ascend from lower states advanced."

This said, they journeyed on in silence, till
They reached the confines of that gloomy land.
And there a mountain capped with murky clouds
Uprose in front and like a barrier stood,
On either hand, prohibiting egress ;
Nor passage seemed to offer nor ascent,
Save by a darksome entrance at the base.

But here the Man, still mindful of the vaults
And of his passage through the dismal halls,
Delayed to enter and besought his Guide
To turn and lead him by some other course.
Then spake the Seraph in reply and said.
"To you the boon is granted to ascend
By other and by lighter way, but see
Thou take good heed and follow me direct,
Lest over-confident in too much light,
Thou lose thy hold and fall in the ascent.
But first the barrier must be removed."
And as he spake a flash of lightning cleft
The murky clouds and smote upon the rocks
And shattered them, that with a crash they fell,
And, bounding, rolled in thunder on the plain,
Disclosing there a narrow stairway formed
Among the rocks, by which ascending soon
They scaled the heights and passed the clouds and
    gained
The seats of men and upper air once more.
But far beyond a glorious land appeared
And shining seas and lakes and happy isles
With flowery fields and choral woods and groves.
And wafted thence upon the air, the sound

Of music and the voice of angels rang
Harmonious and fell upon the ear
And filled the soul with ecstacy divine.
Then taking leave, the Seraph smiling said.
" Now I depart unto the land thou seest,
But stay thou here, complete thy present course
For I shall come and bear thee whence I came,
To isles of light and worlds beyond the sun ! ! "

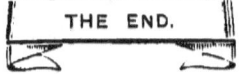

THE END.

PORTEOUS & GIBBS, Printers, Dublin.

THE
CONQUEROR'S DREAM
AND OTHER POEMS.
BY
WM. SHARPE, M.D.

"THE above work, though unpretentious in length, deserves special attention on account of the true poetic feeling evinced in its composition. . . . . . Lofty sentiment and graceful diction characterise it throughout, but they are particularly noticeable in the poem which gives its name to the collection and which is written in blank verse, the most elevated of all measures, and at the same time the most difficult to succeed in, since a correct ear, a delicate taste, and true poetical genius are essential to its perfect development. Dr. Sharpe has proven himself to be in a great degree master of this effective but not easy method of versification. . . . . In the 'Conqueror's Dream' the hollow mockeries of kingly power, and the loneliness of fame is finely shown in an allegorical description of a Warrior's ascent of the summit of ambition, which is pictured under the form of a 'Mighty pile, with domes and towers, and pinnacles, and battlements outspread,' and is designed to represent the edifice of man's progress. . . . . . The picture given of those monarchs who lay upon the topmost height of this tower, 'mere living skeletons all but extinct,' their shrivelled features and their hollow eyes contrasting strangely with their royal robes, is very effective, and none the less so that the picture represents monarchism very much as it exists to-day— intolerable in many of its aspects both to rulers and subjects, but a necessary adjunct of European society, perhaps, in its present state. There are many truths conveyed in the reading of this poem, and the conclusions reached are those of a thoughtful and far-seeing mind. Some of the minor poems, such as 'The Palm Groves' and 'The Warbler and the Bird Collector' are very pleasing, being written in a simple and natural style, which is very delightful. . . . Dr. Sharpe has, besides the qualities we have already enumerated, the clever faculty of never wearying his reader; what he says he utters delicately and expressively, but never at too great length. His thought is vigorous, his language well chosen, and the result is that what he writes is well worthy of attention, and will repay perusal."—*New York Daily Graphic.*

"Dr. Sharpe writes most musically, and his poem on the Palm Groves is perfect as far as it goes. It is moulded, of course, on Mr. Longfellow's 'Hiawatha,' the rythm of which in itself is most attractive, and Dr. Sharpe has put an exquisite picture upon the model. We cannot refrain from quoting a final passage."—*Lloyd's Weekly News.*

" Th   re marked
with a   ld render
them a   uthor is a
devout   on every
page ; a   ed by that
scholarl   nd the ex.
travaga   :am,' is an
admiral   t designed
to conv   iplayed in
the shou   and ' The
Warble   f veritable
gems of

" Sor   d the Bird
Collecte   do almost
Wordsw

" Dr.   ness of his
verse at

" Th   :rue poetic
feeling,   hment — is
flowing

" We   lculated to
delight   '.

" Th   pictures of
the gre   th human
bones."

" Th   ' to appre-
ciate a   iments and
ideas."

" Th   lank verse,
which   iyed in the
reprodu   really the
best th   first poem,
of the   iecially the
passage

" 'T   : length in
blank v   ancies, not
unusua   e of bodily
sufferii   s and their
hollow   rian who is
also a i to ' The
Palm Groves and the Waives and the End the tor,' which
are simple and touching poems of no ordinary merit."—*Public
Opinion.*

London: DAVID BOGUE, 3, St. Martin's Place, W.C.

BY THE SAME AUTHOR.

HUMANITY AND THE MAN.

"There are some very fine passages in this poem; but its humanizing tendency and spirit are its best qualities."—*Public Opinion.*

"It has also a substratum of serious and even often remarkably suggestive thought."—*Literary Churchman.*

"The author has drawn upon his Eastern experience, and describes Eastern scenery, &c., with vividness."—*Peterborough Advertiser.*

"The language and imagery of the poem, which is sometimes Dantesque and sometimes Miltonic in form, are in general dignified and appropriate."—*Limerick Reporter.*

"This is an epic poem which deals with a subject of great interest. . . . The entire is filled with a studied elegance rare in blank verse."—*Londonderry Sentinel.*

"A lofty theme truly: much too high for mere newspaper criticism! It is the vision which in manifold guises has revealed itself more or less brightly to star-gazers of all generations."—*Bradford Daily Observer.*

"There is much sound thinking and elevated sentiment in the poem, the versification of which seems moulded on that of Milton's immortal epic."—*Warwick Advertiser.*

"The work displays no small amount of knowledge, whilst its philosophy is highly commendable, and further interesting volumes may fairly be expected from so able a pen."—*Birmingham Daily Gazette.*

"We have treated at some length Dr. Sharpe's poem, because, setting aside many obvious imperfections, the work is a masterly production and one we can recommend to our readers with the greatest confidence."—*Hampshire Telegraph.*

DUBLIN: HODGES, FOSTER, AND FIGGIS.
LONDON: SIMPKIN, MARSHALL, AND CO.